THE GRAY LION

JOEY OLIVER

DEFIANCE PRESS
& PUBLISHING

The Gray Lion

ISBN-13: 978-1-955937-35-1 (Paperback)
ISBN-13: 978-1-955937-34-4 (eBook)

Published by Defiance Press and Publishing, LLC

Bulk orders of this book may be obtained by contacting Defiance Press and Publishing, LLC. www.defiancepress.com.

Public Relations Dept. – Defiance Press & Publishing, LLC
281-581-9300
pr@defiancepress.com

Defiance Press & Publishing, LLC
281-581-9300
info@defiancepress.com

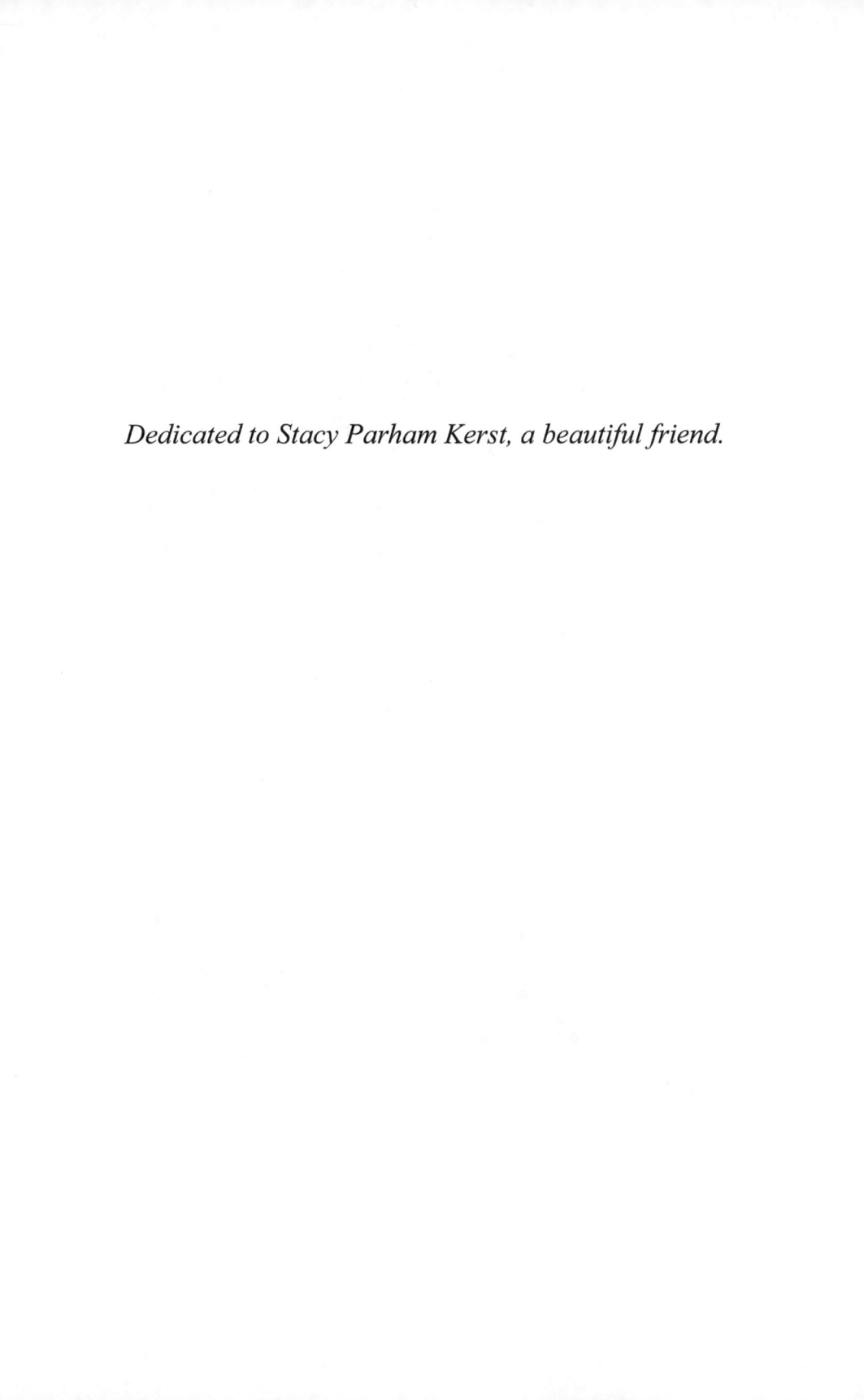

Dedicated to Stacy Parham Kerst, a beautiful friend.

Nymean Peninsula

Aspero Ocean

Borens

Acton

Norston

Barain Islands

Cophina

Northern Cluster

Casgardian Mountains

Valgard

Dalwen

Shoria

✗
Capital

Galgaria

Polissa

Grastian
✗

Alderia

Malshire

Fort Malum

✗ Arcem

Tenebris River

PART I

CHAPTER 1

"I told you to stop swinging like that Kain!"

"I thought you said you've gotten quicker Bruce!" Kain shouted out while slashing his wooden sword against his brother's.

"This isn't how Ben wants us to fight!" Bruce whined. He then gritted his teeth and struck back.

"I'm just having a little fun." Kain responded, shaking his head and rolling his eyes.

The two boys' blades continued to clash back and forth against each other. As Kain's swings sped up, Bruce kept getting pushed further and further back. He was trying to parry the blows as best as he could, but it was taking everything in him to block the strikes coming his way.

As Kain kept a flurry of slashes coming from all directions, he looked down at his brother's feet and noticed he was quickly losing his balance. Kain swiped his sword across Bruce's shoulder, but Bruce sidestepped just as Kain's sword came crashing down. While Kain was still exposed, Bruce took a swipe at his head. Kain dropped to his knee, and Bruce's slash came just over his head. Kain leapt up and returned the very same blow to the side of his brother's skull.

"Ahhh!" Bruce screamed. He dropped his sword and moved both of his hands up to his ear. Kain took a step back and let his sword hang at his side. Bruce turned back to Kain, growled, and then lunged at him. The boys rolled around wrestling in the meadow grass as Bruce pounded his fists into his brother.

"Hey, what's going on?" a man called out from across the prairie. He was now jogging over after hearing the boys' screams. He grabbed the two young boys and separated them from each other. Bruce was holding his head while he glared at Kain.

Bruce turned to the man and cried out, "Uncle Ben, Kain whacked me in the head! And he isn't fighting how you showed us." Kain stood there silently with his arms crossed.

Ben sighed and rubbed his face; he looked down at the two boys and rested his hands on his hips. His loosely fitting shirt blew gently in the wind. Ben scratched his short, brown beard and pulled his hair back.

"You need to learn to be careful with these," Ben stated firmly. "They're not supposed to be toys. And if you really want to become a great swordsman like you say Kain, you need to focus on the fundamentals." Ben's eyes were locked with his nephew's.

"But I'm sick of all these slow training exercises. I want to fight!" Kain sliced his sword through the air. He looked up at his uncle and pleaded, "When am I going to be ready? This isn't even a challenge for us anymore. I can do everything you've shown me! I—I want a real battle!" Kain slouched his shoulders and dropped his hands.

Ben took a deep breath before answering, "You're quite far away from that day, Kain. Even those as talented as your father had to go through these exact same training exercises. You need to put the time in. I promise you, one day it will serve you more than you could ever imagine." Ben knelt next to his young nephew and put his hand on his shoulder. Kain met Ben's gaze with a frown still frozen on his face.

"The names of all those immortalized fighters you've heard throughout your life—did you ever think about how they became what they did? Success is very often one of, if not the last thing you achieve, and it always comes after many failures. And many, many days of wanting to simply give up." Ben paused for a moment. "I know how you feel, wishing you could skip all of that and just have it now, the glory, the skills. I can see it in your eyes. But I'll tell you the secret." Ben stood back up and stared out at the setting sun. "If you can manage to keep that look in your eyes, no matter what difficulty lies in your way. If you can manage to keep going, day after day, eventually … you will achieve what you seek. That I can promise." Kain looked up solemnly at his uncle. The sun's rays lit up his golden-brown hair as he stared at Ben. "But that's enough training for today; come inside. Your mother said she has dinner ready."

Kain sheathed his wooden sword on his hip and followed his uncle and brother through the meadow. As they passed through the fields, the sun was closing in on the horizon behind them. Their small cottage sat in solitude along the edge of the forest line. Crops surrounded the property almost entirely except for a small dirt pathway that led up to the entrance of the shack. A small shed with a few goats, chickens and pigs stood beside the hut. The three boys walked along the dirt path and soon reached the front door of their home. The boys' mother, Meredith, stood beside the table placing wooden cups along the edges.

"Are you hungry boys? I've just taken the porridge off the fire." Meredith asked as she grabbed a stack of bowls from the cupboard. She heard a resounding *yes*. The boys sat down and watched while she set the four bowls around the table. She pushed her long, blond hair away from her face as she scooped the meal out of the pot. When she glanced up, her hand froze. She set the ladle down and started making her way over to the other side of the table.

"Bruce, what's that on your head?" Meredith sounded both angry and worried. She was staring at the small stream of dried blood above Bruce's ear.

"Kain hit me," Bruce mumbled as he looked over at his brother and scowled.

"Here we go …" Kain moaned and slapped the table.

Meredith whipped her head over to Ben and shrieked, "You already know how I feel about you teaching them to fight, and now you let this happen?" She grabbed Bruce's head, pushed up his blond hair and inspected the lump that was slowly beginning to grow above his ear. She grabbed a rag and began wiping away the red crust.

"Well, they're going to miss every now and then." Ben whispered before casually sipping his soup, trying to hide a slight smile.

Meredith hit Ben on the shoulder and then continued berating him, "You always say this training is for their safety, but what about when that's not a wooden sword, Ben!" Meredith paused as tears began to swell in her eyes. She gasped for breath as she whispered, "I can't … I can't lose them. Not like Victor." She clutched her chest and threw her rag down. "I don't want them doing this anymore. That's it." Meredith shook her head and put her hand to her forehead.

"Meredith," Ben said softly as he grabbed his sister's arm. "I'll never let that happen. I made that promise to him years ago. My sole mission in life would be to protect you, Kain and Bruce if anything were to happen to him. And unfortunately," Ben stared at the ground, "he is gone. But believe me, there's nothing in this world that could make me break that promise." The table fell silent as the two young boys looked up at their mother. Meredith quickly regained her composure. She took a deep breath and put her hands on her hips while keeping her gaze focused on the table.

Meredith then slammed the rag down and said, "Right, well, when you've finished your meals, Kain and Ben, you guys can clean all this up. Bruce, come with me and we'll wash that off; you need a good scrub anyway."

The last remaining light from the sunset had now vanished, and after the dishes were removed from the table, Ben walked over to the hearth to begin a fire. As he sat crouched beside the fireplace,

Kain came over and stood behind him. Kain was looking up above the fireplace at a sword mounted on the wall. The flames of the fire now flickered along the bronze blade.

"Ben," Kain said quietly. "Was my father really as great a warrior as you say?" Ben turned back to Kain, and then he moved his eyes up to the sword.

"Your father …" Ben shook his head slowly as he answered. "Was one of the greatest fighters this land has seen in many, many years." Kain looked down at his feet.

"Why did he die then?" Kain said under his breath. His lip began to quiver as he held back tears. Ben sat quietly for a moment before standing up. He reached out his hand, took the sword off the mantle and admired the gleam of the blade. The flames danced mystically against it.

"If you want to know the story of how your father died, you must first know the truth of how your father lived." Ben said with a smile. He looked down at Kain and raised his eyebrows. "The whole truth." Ben gazed into the eyes of the young boy while slowly swinging the sword back and forth. "Your mother would prefer that you continue to live in ignorance, and that you and your brother remain here all your life, living quietly as farmers … as a family. But she can't protect you forever. You will both grow up one day; that I can assure you. And your time will come. It's inevitable." Ben started to pace back and forth around the room. "Victor grew up in the same village as me and your mother—Shoria. It's not far from here, a few hours ride south is all. But those were very different times on the peninsula. When we were young men, the Kingdom that now rules our lands was undergoing a great deal of turmoil. As you well know, the entire Nymean peninsula wasn't always controlled by the crown. In fact, it wasn't until I was a young man that the King had grown his Kingdom and finally conquered all the northern and western villages. But it was not without a great military cost to them, and not without earning the disdain of nearly all that had been conquered. The outer villages had fought hard against the crown for years, and they long opposed the King's crusade. But, in the end, we failed to defeat them." Ben looked at the ground and bit his cheek. "Well, after a few years of being under their control, the King decided he wanted to bring a sense of unification to all of the people that lived throughout his land. He sent his newly appointed Royal Hand to lead an occupation of the outer villages. To teach us their ways." Ben laughed and stared into the fire. "When the King's men arrived at our village, they quickly began to make their … proclamations. First, they demanded their troops be quartered. We didn't really even think anything of it. It seemed like a small price to pay, just helping the soldiers who were passing through our town. Well, we didn't realize they would be staying. Foolish we were. Next, they demanded they be fed the premium food supply from our farms. Soon their hunger began to take priority over our citizens and even our own children. Yet still, we gave in. Not long after our first concession, every aspect of our lives then became infected with these cretins. Inch by inch they took over. Months went by and the native villagers were continuously being tormented, raped, and starved. We lived life in a constant state of fear each day while these soldiers took every chance they could to abuse us. We had no idea what could be done about it. You see, many men were just glad to simply be alive after the wars. So you could say our fight had run out by then." Kain looked up at his uncle intensely as he recreated the scenes in his head. Ben stoked the flames of the hearth with the sword before continuing, "People can put up with a lot you know." He glanced over at Kain then quickly turned back to face the fire. "On an individual level at least. And we certainly did. But after a few months, the King eventually overplayed his hand of authority. He made his most demanding declaration, that all the boys in the village were to be rounded up and taken to join the Royal Army." Ben raised an eyebrow, "They needed to rebuild you see. Their forces had been worn thin at the conclusion of the wars." Ben then bent down into a squatting position. "When you go after people's children, Kain, the whole rules of the game change. The whole rules of life change. People suddenly aren't so willing to submit just to make things a little bit easier for themselves. These parents were willing to die for their sons. And their outrage, which had already begun to boil, soon blew its top. But what really sealed the King's fate, unexpectedly happened to be his demand that immediately followed. His second proclamation of the day, declared that we now owed the Kingdom any and all excess food we produced, as a loyalty tax in order to feed their newly attained soldiers that were soon to be living all the way out in the Capital. Not much of a benefit on our end." Ben looked over at Kain and smiled. "Now, your grandfather was the best farmer in the village, and this tax meant he would lose everything he had worked so hard to build. All of his wealth, gone. And so, he refused. He burned his crop fields before they could take it from him." Ben smiled once more. "God damn your grandfather ..." He shook his head. "Well, for this refusal, he was hanged, drawn and quartered in the village square. And when they asked him to give his last words, he just spat in the executioner's face." Kain's eyes opened wide. "But ... Victor had been away that evening. When he returned that night and saw his father's corpse left to rot in the streets, he swore that would be the final night of the King's reign over him. He gathered up all the men in the town who had fought with him in the wars against the King. He asked for our help to fight. Most of the men had children of their own, and they were now more than willing to fight in order to save their sons from such a fate. They all agreed. And then we planned our assault. Just before daybreak, we attacked. These military men may have been bullies, but they were weak. A bunch of young fodder for the front lines. Dress up soldiers. Unlike them, we had seen a real war. We had seen the horror of the battlefields after hours of metal hacking into flesh. We weren't scared. We were inspired. We had nothing to lose, and we were dangerous. It didn't take long for us to free the town. We slayed every soldier in that village, but it didn't stop there. Our fight had sparked a rebellion. Your father and the rest of us began traveling from town to town, freeing the people in the outer villages of their military occupation. Word began spreading of these uprisings, and the King began to lose his grip on his newly expanded Kingdom. For the next few weeks, our numbers grew dramatically. For every man we lost in battle, at least two more came and joined the cause. We had grown far stronger than anything the Kingdom could've imagined, and once we had the strength and size, we marched on the Capital."

"Did you go too? Did you attack the Capital?" Kain felt butterflies in his stomach.

Ben laughed and stared down at his nephew before answering, "No, I did not. I was under strict orders from your father. I was to return home and keep your pregnant mother safe!" He patted Kain on the back and gave a sad smile.

"What happened when my father took on the Capital?" Kain blurted out. Ben then sighed and dropped his head slightly. After a few moments of silence, he looked to the ceiling and shut his eyes.

Ben continued, "Just as Victor prepared to take the Capital, he and his men were ambushed. Your father had … put his faith in the wrong men. You see, early on during the rebellion, your father had made alliances with many of the nobles throughout the peninsula. At first, they had seemed almost as inspired by the rebellion as we were. And at times they truly did help us in winning crucial battles. Bringing men from throughout the outer villages to help. But …" Ben put his hands over his face. "But, they were still men. And like all, well, most men, they had their price. They were bought off by the King. Promised land and riches if they could only manage to bring your father and his men close enough to the Kingdom so that the King could gather the full strength of his army and then take them by surprise. And, that's what happened." Ben kept his gaze stuck to the fire. "The night before Victor planned to take the Capital, they were all … slaughtered in the night. They never saw it coming. Your father and his most loyal men were captured, lined up above the city square and executed. Their heads were staked on the four corners of the city walls, and those 'nobles', as they claimed to be …" Ben let out a disgusted scoff. "Basked in their rewards while they watched from the crowd as your father and his men were tortured and murdered." Kain stared blankly into the shine of his father's sword. Ben then grinned proudly, "But, I can promise you, this Kingdom won't forget the name of Victor Villairo for a long, long time. Word has it that King Alastor still fears his name to this day."

"I think that's enough." The sound of Meredith's voice made Kain jump. He snapped his head over and saw his mother standing in the kitchen with her arms resting on Bruce's shoulder. Her glare pierced through Ben. "It's time for you boys to go to bed. All three of you."

As the boys climbed the ladder up to their bed, Ben pulled Meredith aside and argued in a hushed tone, "It was time they knew. You can't keep them locked up here forever."

"Yes, I can." Meredith stated as she finished wringing out her wet washrag. "I won't let them share his fate. And if someone finds out they're his sons …."

"How would anyone find out? Neither of them know any of the local children, and no one here would remember you from Shoria."

Meredith closed her eyes and took a deep breath as she whispered, "We just need to be as careful as possible."

"We will be." Ben promised.

CHAPTER 2

When morning came, Ben and Meredith tended to their crops, and the boys went out to practice their daily training routine at the edge of the prairie. After a few hours had gone by, Kain started to get bored.

"Let's go into the forest. We haven't been to the river in so long." Kain clasped his hands together and urged his brother to agree to come.

Bruce looked down at the ground before answering, "I don't know. You know Ben and Mom don't like us going off the farm."

"Come on Bruce. It's not a big deal. Let's go. Just to the river. They'll be busy all day with their crops."

Bruce stood silently for a moment, and then rolled his eyes slightly. "Alright, fine. But just to the river." Kain smiled mischievously as him and Bruce began their journey through the tree line. They walked along the natural paths of the sparse forest. Autumn leaves had just begun falling and the sun's rays glistened through the canopy. The boys strolled along with their wooden swords hanging at their waists. It didn't take long for them to reach the creek. As they glanced downstream along the river's edge, they saw a young girl filling a cauldron of water about fifty feet away. "Woah," Bruce said under his breath.

The girl looked up, seemingly unstartled. She tucked her short, amber hair behind her ear and calmly called out, "Hello Kain."

"Alice! I … didn't expect to see you here. I, uh …" Kain's voice was shaky. He scratched the back of his neck as he searched for the next thing to say. Nothing came to him.

"So is this your brother Bruce then?" The young girl asked in a quiet voice while she held her cauldron in the stream.

"Yeah, we were coming down here to do a little training," Kain replied as he proudly grabbed his sword.

Alice stood from the river's edge and responded, "Well, after I drop this off at my house, I'm going to go into town to sell some wool. I could use some help carrying it if you guys would like to join me."

"Yeah we would!" Kain yelled back.

"Kain! We aren't supposed to go into town …" Bruce hissed through clenched teeth.

"Fine then Bruce. You can go home." Kain said, turning his head and glaring at his brother.

"If it's any trouble—"

"It's not!" Kain assured Alice. "Me and you will go, and Bruce can stay back."

Bruce sulked away while looking uneasy about his brother's disobedience. Kain took no notice of it and ran over to Alice. The two headed back through the forest toward her house.

"You know, you don't look anything like your brother," Alice mentioned as she looked over at Kain. "Didn't you say he was your twin?"

"Oh, yeah … we're twins but not the kind that look the same." Kain said, looking slightly uncomfortable. Alice stared at Kain's wooden sword on his hip.

"So, if you guys aren't the same …" Alice then glanced up at Kain. "Which of you is the better fighter?" She asked.

Kain quickly gripped his hilt and answered, "Definitely me. I'm a lot faster than Bruce. He likes to play defense, but I like to attack." He drew his sword and stabbed at the air. Alice smiled and stared down at the cauldron resting against her stomach.

Soon the two kids were out of the woods and had reached Alice's home. Once Alice dropped her cauldron off, she and Kain loaded up a few baskets of wool and then followed the road into town. As they reached the outskirts of the village, they noticed an old woman in the distance slowly walking toward them along the dirt path. Her spine had been twisted and bent by the weight of time. A blue robe covered most of her body and head, with only a wrinkled and leathery face creeping out of her oversized hood.

"Alice, I was on my way out here to come and see your mother. What are you doing heading into town?" The old woman shouted from up the road.

"Hi Grandmother. Me and Kain were coming into town to deliver this wool." Alice's grandmother nodded before turning her attention to Kain.

"I haven't seen you around, boy. What was your name again?" The old woman asked in a gruff and shrill voice.

"My name's Kain. I don't come into town much. My mother doesn't really let me."

The grandmother cranked her head before responding, "Your mother doesn't let you into town … what are you, a part of that pagan commune out by the cliffs?"

"No …?" Kain was confused. "She just, doesn't want me coming into town is all."

"And what is your family name, young Kain?" The old woman questioned Kain while gently stroking her chin.

"Villairo. And my mother is—"

"Meredith?" The grandmother interjected as her eyes opened wide. "Your mother … is Meredith Villairo?" She gasped. "So it is true then!" The grandmother's eye began to twitch. She stared maniacally at Kain. After a brief pause, her mouth twisted and formed a cruel smile. "Well, it was so *very* wonderful to meet you Kain … Villairo." She bowed her already crouched head and continued trudging along toward Alice's house.

Later that evening, Kain made his way back home. Luckily, Bruce had fed a story to their mother about Kain deciding to build a fort in the forest to explain why he had been gone all day. On his way back through the farm, Kain walked by Ben and Meredith milking their goats in the shed.

Ben looked up and yelled out as Kain walked by, "Build a decent fort then Kain?"

"What?" Kain halted. "Oh, uh, yeah … pretty good." He stood there for a minute, watching his mother and uncle. After being pleasantly surprised that they were not at all suspicious, he quickly headed inside.

Ben and Meredith came in soon after Kain and then started to set the table for dinner. As he hung his sweater up, Ben looked down at the plate of food on the table.

Ben sighed before he announced, "We only have bread for dinner tonight boys. Your mother needs to go into town tomorrow to get some more flint for the fire. And tomorrow I'll be out fishing most of the day. Hopefully I can make up for this lousy meal." The four of them sat down around the table. "So Kain, how's your fort looking?" Ben glanced over at Kain and bit off a chunk of bread.

"What?" Kain's eyes widened as he put his hands flat on the table.

Ben restated, "You know, the fort you've been building all day." Kain nervously looked around the room until Bruce kicked him in the shin.

"Ah! The fort. Yeah it's coming along pretty well. It's really big, very complex. It might be my best one yet. It's taken me all day. I'm working on getting enough ferns to actually make the roof now, but I'm close to finishing it. Hopefully it manages to stay up through the night." Kain bit his cheek as he tried to hold in his smile. Ben swallowed his food and nodded; then he set his bread down and wiped the crumbs from his face.

"Maybe we can all go check it out tomorrow once you've finished and I get back from fishing." Ben said while smiling at his nephew warmly.

Kain felt his stomach drop. He rubbed his neck as he responded, "Well, I'm probably going to just take it down once I'm done. I don't want it to attract any … uh … dangerous animals." Kain was bouncing his knee and staring down at his food.

Ben tilted his head and frowned. "That doesn't really seem like all that much of a concern, I think you'll be fine to keep it up. I'm excited to see it."

Kain nodded slowly and looked down at his plate of food. Bruce was desperately looking back and forth between his mother and uncle.

"Kain." The piercing voice of his mother made Kain twitch. Meredith had been staring at him with squinted eyes. "Is that a sunburn on your face?" Both the bridge of Kain's nose and his cheeks were bright pink.

"Uh …" Kain's mouth had fallen open slightly while he tried to come up with something to say.

"You built the fort in the forest, right?" Meredith asked.

"Yes." Kain's face ran hot as he felt his mother's stare inspecting him.

"Hard to get a sunburn under those trees, don't you think?"

Kain scrunched his face and answered, "Me and Bruce were practicing until about noon in the prairie; I bet it was from that." He chewed on his bread.

"Bruce doesn't have a sunburn." Meredith said as she crossed her arms.

Bruce was sitting across the table and glaring at Kain. He knew if

Kain's excuses didn't work, he'd be in just as much trouble for lying.

Kain rolled his eyes and looked around the room before responding, "I don't know Mom. I guess the sun gets through the leaves. Not much I can do about it." Kain scarfed down the rest of his bread and with a full mouth said, "Look I'm pretty tired from all that building today. I think I'm gonna try and go to sleep." Meredith and Ben glanced over at each other.

After a long pause, Meredith uncrossed her arms and broke the silence, "Fine, both of you clean up the table and then go to bed."

Kain shot up and started grabbing the plates from everyone. Bruce pulled a rag out from a bucket of water and wiped the table down. Once they finished, the two boys climbed up the ladder to the attic and went to sleep.

CHAPTER 3

Meredith departed for the village early the following morning carrying a pouch of eggs by her side. Once she had made her way into the interior of the dense cluster of huts, she went immediately to the blacksmith shop. After pushing open the door and hearing the soft entry bell ring, she walked up to the counter.

"How much for a flint stick?" Meredith asked.

The older man behind the counter had a stoic look on his blackened, dirty face. He rested his hands on the desk while his large belly pressed up against it.

"Well, what do you have?" The man answered while keeping a blank expression.

"I have these." Meredith then laid her pouch of eggs on the desk.

The man stared at them for a moment, looking unimpressed. He then shrugged his shoulders slightly and decided, "Yeah, this'll do." He started picking up each of the ten eggs.

"All ten?" Meredith was stunned at such a price.

"Do you want the flint or not woman?"

Meredith clenched her jaw and agreed. She put the flint into her pouch and headed out of the shack. As she stepped out of the shop, she was blasted backward by a gust of wind. A pack of cavalry men had ridden right in front of her. Soldiers from the King's army were now making their way into the town square where a crowd of villagers had begun to gather. Meredith stood outside of the blacksmith shop and watched as the massive and menacing Royal Hand of Nymea dismounted from his black stallion. The other soldiers assembled behind him. Meredith hesitantly started walking toward the crowd. She raised the hood of her forest green cloak over her head.

The booming voice of the Royal Hand began to echo through the town, "Men and women of Valgard, the Kingdom of Nymea is facing resistance as we expand our lands. Tensions are persisting, even rising. If this does indeed result in a war, I assure you all that Nymea will prevail. But, in preparation, we will be needing a significant amount of cooperation from our villages. Firstly, your farms will need to contribute double the amount of grain that is usually required. This is to keep our troops strong and full. Secondly, all metal work will be directed toward the furnishment of arrow tips, to be collected weekly. And the third and final proclamation by your King Alastor … all boys between the ages of eleven and twenty-two will be required to join our military ranks. War may be coming soon, and we must have a strong army at the ready. Remember, this is all being done for the personal protection of each of you." Protesting cries immediately filled the town square after the announcement. The King's Hand responded coldly as he turned his back to the crowd, "Give them up now, or we will take them by force. Doesn't matter to me." He walked back to his horse as soldiers stepped forward and seized any young boys throughout the crowd.

Meredith stood there, frozen. Her hands began to tremble as she thought of her young sons. She had kept Kain and Bruce a secret all these years for this exact reason. She could only hope the King's men would not begin raiding houses in search of any other boys in hiding. She selfishly prayed the village parents would go along with this willingly. If there was enough compliance, the soldiers may not even have a reason to raid houses. But she couldn't make an assumption like that. She thought it would be safest to go home and hide the two boys. She began backing away from the crowd slowly. Soldiers were inhabiting nearly every alleyway at this point. She had to figure out how to avoid the soldiers or she would undoubtedly be questioned about her family. Once Meredith had reached the edge of the crowd, she spun around and saw an old, weathered finger pointed right at her face.

"Meredith Villairo." The woman's insidious smile was creeping out from beneath her hood. "I believe you have a son to give up." Her voice rang in Meredith's ears.

Meredith froze once more. Her eyes then widened. She realized she had known the old woman many years ago. The woman had been a seamstress in Shoria when Meredith was a young girl. How the old woman knew about one of her sons, she had no idea.

Meredith backed away with her arms stretched out; her face remained fixed in a state of panic. She turned and ran from the old woman, desperately looking between alleyways for a safe escape route out of the village. Behind her she could hear the woman screaming at the guards.

"Stop her! She has a son! That's Meredith Villairo. Her boy is the child of Victor Villairo!" Anyone who heard the claim coming from the old woman immediately looked over in the direction of the commotion. Soldiers then spotted the fleeing Meredith and chased after her.

"Old woman! What did you say?" The Royal Hand's voice boomed throughout the village. He was now marching over toward Alice's grandmother. She looked up at the iron-clad soldier towering over her and spoke.

"That woman was once the wife of Victor Villairo. They both grew up in Shoria, where I lived during and before the Great Rebellion. Some of us had heard the rumors of Victor fathering a child before his death, but it was only whispers. Until yesterday, I believed her to be a childless widow who lived out on one of the farms with whom I believe is her brother. She would come into town every so often for supplies, but I never thought very much of it. I mean, I had always thought she looked familiar, but it was my granddaughter who befriended her son, Kain. And yesterday, I saw him. Then I remembered her! She *was* Victor Villairo's wife! They must have had a child before he died. And she's been hiding him; she doesn't let him go into town for fear he will be noticed. I wouldn't be surprised if she didn't even know he and my little Alice were friends." There was a slight pause. "He even looks like him too …" The old woman's voice trailed off.

The King's Hand squinted down at the old woman and put his fist to his chin. After a few moments of silence, he finally spoke, "And where is this farm?"

Meredith had finally succeeded in evading the search of the men on her tail. After gaining some separation from the soldiers, she slipped away into the forest that bordered the village. She managed to make the detoured trek all the way home without being followed. Once she was back at her house, Meredith burst through the door and found Kain and Bruce sitting at the table playing with small clay toys. She was overwhelmed with relief and ran up to hug them. As she held them, Bruce pointed to the window.

"Mom, look," Bruce said with his finger outstretched. Meredith twisted her head around to see three soldiers racing toward the house on horseback.

Meredith warned her sons, "Quickly, we need to hide. And don't make a sound."

There was a stowaway hatch near the back of the house where Meredith put Bruce into. Between the walls beside the fireplace there was a gap where she shoved Kain into. After being unable to find a proper hiding place for herself and with time running out, Meredith decided to stuff herself into the storage space along with Bruce.

The three soldiers busted open the door. They crept inside and scanned the room. After briefly browsing the small shack, they saw no sign of life.

"Hey, look at this," one of the soldiers said as he picked up a clay figurine sitting on the table. "Guess that old woman was right. It seems there was a kid here."

"I'll bet they made a run for it by now," another soldier added.

Ben was walking through the prairie with his basket of fish slung over his back. As he approached the house, he noticed the three military horses stationed outside. The door of the hut was also open wide. He crept up to the house and peeked through the window. He could hear murmurs about a 'boy.' He paused, took a deep breath, and then headed inside while trying to appear as innocent as possible. He walked through the doorway holding a basket of fish by his side. The men immediately turned to him.

Ben addressed the three intruders, "Soldiers, what is it you're doing here?" He set his basket of fish down by the fireplace and put his hands on his hips. The soldiers drew their swords and swarmed Ben.

"We know about the boy. And you must be the uncle, yes?" The soldiers had lost their relaxed attitude and were now glaring at Ben.

"Uncle? No, no. I'm Meredith's neighbor. I help her with her crops sometimes. Look, I brought her some fish." Ben assured the invaders. He then pointed to his fish basket as one of the guards smacked him in the face with the flat of his blade. Ben fell to the ground. He rubbed his face before staggering to his knees.

"Well, where is she then … neighbor?" The soldier taunted as he stared down at Ben. The man showed a phony smile and then cocked his head to the right. Another soldier crouched down to meet Ben's eyeline.

"I … I don't know. Did she do something wrong?" Ben asked, but the soldiers weren't convinced of his supposed ignorance. One of them pulled out a bullwhip and cracked it across Ben's back.

"Where is the fucking boy!" The soldiers shout sent shivers down Kain's spine. Ben shrieked in pain as the whip lashed across his back.

After continued silence from Ben, one soldier suggested, "Maybe we should just kill him." The other soldier stood as he continued to scowl at Ben.

The soldier rubbed his face and replied, "That's not a bad idea. I really don't have the energy to interrogate him right now." The man then gripped his sword tightly and readied for a swing.

Kain watched in pure desperation through a crack between the walls. His heart was pounding out of his chest. A flood of anger consumed him as he watched his uncle being treated like an animal. The man raised his sword, but before he could strike, Kain had stormed out from his hiding place and tried to tackle the soldier.

"There he is!" The three men yelled out as they picked up Kain. He shrieked and flailed. They started to laugh as they restrained him. "Well, the King sure will be happy about this one." As he was being pulled away, Kain looked back and saw the eyes of his brother Bruce looking helplessly at him through the cracks in the floorboard. Meredith held Bruce tightly with her hand over his mouth. Tears streamed down her face.

"It's going to be alright Kain!" Ben called out desperately while he was whipped across the face one more time. He fell back onto the ground as Kain was brought outside.

The soldiers stuck Kain on the back of one of their horses and headed for the village. Kain stared back at his home while metal shackles held his hands and feet. He shut his eyes. Small tears dripped down his cheeks.

Once Kain and the soldiers arrived at the town square, Kain was stuffed into one of the carriages which were now filled with the rounded-up boys in the village as well as those from the other towns that the army had already passed through. Hundreds of young men and boys stared blankly through their cages at the new batch of recruits from Valgard. A solemn silence radiated from them. Kain felt the weight of the world pulling on him by his restraints.

One of the soldiers who had seen the previous drama ensue walked over to the King's Hand. The soldier bowed his head and addressed the Royal Hand, "My Lord." The King's Hand nodded in approval while admiring the gauntlet on his left hand. He towered over the soldier at six-foot-four-inches tall. His shoulders were broad, twice that of a normal man, with tree trunk legs holding him up. His short, black beard roughened his square face. The soldier looked up at him and asked, "Is that really the son of Victor Villairo?" The King's Hand glanced over at Kain as he was being forced into the carriage. The King's Hand narrowed his eyes and frowned. His gaze was fixed on the boy.

"We'll soon find out. Load the rest of them up. We'll start our journey back to the Capital tonight." The King's Hand ordered. The soldier then scurried off to help secure the rest of the boys. He latched the last remaining carriage to their horses and began preparing for them to leave.

"Soldiers, move out!" The Royal Hand commanded once he saw the fleet was prepared.

The carriages were jam packed. There was hardly any open-air space. Kain was tucked in the corner with his face pressed up against the rope fencing. He stared back at Valgard, and ever so slowly, the sight of the town began to fade into the distance. The stoic silence of the boys in the carriages and the repetitive clanking of the soldiers' armor beside him began to make him drowsy. Soon he fell asleep, hoping he would eventually wake from this nightmare.

CHAPTER 4

The blinding light of the sunrise abruptly brought Kain back to his new reality. He was now staring upon the gleaming white castle walls of the Capital. Guardsmen and archers occupied each of the watchtowers that stood fifty feet apart from each other. The front facade of the castle stretched almost as far as Kain could see. He had never even imagined that something of this size could exist.

"Let down the door!" a man yelled from atop the tower as the army approached. "Looks like we got ourselves that new batch of soldiers! Get these boys all set up, eh!"

Kain was so nervous he hardly noticed the dried sweat and various body parts pressing into him. Once the door to the castle finally reached the ground, the army began to squeeze its way inside. Merchants lined their makeshift shops while residents looked to trade, but as soon as the army made its way through the streets, the citizens cleared out. The carriages were the first to pass through the streets of the Capital. People stood aside, staring at the caged boys like they were zoo animals.

After passing through what appeared to be the main market strip, the carriages then continued forward into the castle square. It was a massive open area, and to the east sat a balcony nearly thirty feet off the ground. Towering behind the balcony appeared to be the King's palace. A grand staircase in the middle of the balcony led to a golden podium that stood just before the massive entrance to the palace. The palace itself was a giant trapezoid with gold trimming along the edges. Four cement rods protruded from each corner of the structure. All the masonry in the city was crafted in pristine white sandstone. The entirety of the city shone a magnificent white gleam except for the tiles of cobblestone that made up the ground. They were blood red.

"Alright, unload them!" The King's Hand called out to the army as he slid from the back of his horse.

Soldiers began cutting the ropes that restrained the cages, and the boys filed out into the square. Even still, the boys stayed silent. All nervously huddled around each other so as not to be identified as an outsider of the herd. Kain was soon being pushed to the outer edge as everyone subtly tried their best to hide. He desperately looked for a way back into the safety of anonymity as the more juvenile soldiers started to circle the boys.

"This is gonna be a fun bunch, ain't it Daren?" One of the circling soldiers shouted.

"They're looking extra fresh this time around. These westerners really have a different feel to them! Nothing like the northerner boys." The other soldier yelled back with a devious smile on his face. The two of them looked like hyenas stalking prey. A cold chill ran down Kain's spine as he gulped. He could hardly breathe. His heart was beating so fast he could feel the pulsations in his ears. He had never felt more exposed in his life as he continued to be nudged further and further to the edge of the circle.

Suddenly, the soldiers fell silent and instantly shifted into form. They stood at attention and immediately looked up toward the royal podium. A squadron of eight men wearing golden bronze armor from head to toe marched over to the podium in a circular formation. Within their huddle, all that could be seen between their strides was a blood red shroud. When they reached the center of the podium, the guardsmen fell back perfectly in line.

Out of the formation came a man with a startlingly pale face. The stark whiteness of his skin was sharply contrasted against his red robes. His eyes were pinched in closer to each other than a normal man's. His eyebrows had thinned out to the point where they were hardly even visible, but it was his cold, stale face that was most startling, for it looked as if it had never felt the feeling of true joy. Above his slicked back, gray and black, greasy hair sat a thin, golden crown.

The King began to make his announcement, "Welcome, welcome! Nymea's newest soldiers. I foresee you all being brave and valiant defenders of the crown. Your Kingdom thanks you for your service." He then gave a slight bow along with a phony, wicked smile. "I can assure you that we will make soldiers out of each and every one of you." The King clasped his hands together and began pacing back and forth beside the podium. "Soon, you will be divided by age, and sent to your respective training facilities. You will be housed in the barracks, and each will be assigned an instructor. Training will be … difficult … gruesome, some have even said. However, this is what it takes to assure that Nymea has only the soldiers that are the most capable and worthy defenders of these lands. And now, I turn these boys back to you, Sir Drake."

The King's Hand nodded, uncrossed his arms and instructed, "Alright boys, break yourselves up. Eleven-year-olds down here, twenty-two-year-olds over here. Everyone else, fill in the gaps. And make it quick!" The boys shyly made their way into their proper group-ings. Soft mumbling broke out as they started to sort themselves into the correct age groups. Kain cautiously walked over to the group of eleven-year-olds that was forming. "Commanders, take these boys to their barracks, get them dressed right, and then bring them back to the training facilities." Upon hearing the orders from Drake, the army dissipated. The groups of boys then began following each of their assigned leaders. Drake made his way up the stairs to meet with the King.

"It appears you've brought us a solid group of boys," The King said as Drake reached the top of the steps. Drake bowed.

"My Lord, yes I agree. They do look somewhat promising. God knows we'll need some capable soldiers in the coming years." Drake replied. He then stood upright and the two started to walk together.

The King tilted his head upward before responding, "I have news regarding the conflicts we are facing. I believe we will fortunately be having some comfort in the near future. Discussions with the Tantian and Alderian Kingdoms have gone over well in recent days. It is really only the Galgarians that I'm concerned with now. Tensions are indeed rising. But, if it is a war they want, then they will surely get it." His expression turned cold and dark. He paused, then turned, shrugged his shoulders and smiled at Drake. "Besides, all the more reason to rebuild our army." The King and Drake started walked down the stairs from the balcony to the city square.

"Well then, the boys must be just about ready for their little, initiation ceremony," the King said with a sly smile. "Why don't we head over and watch? It's always my favorite part."

On the other side of the castle, Kain was almost finished being fitted with a chest plate and arm guards. Once he was properly fitted, he was then given a wooden sword. He was ordered to stand outside his barrack as soon as he was dressed. He then slowly peeked beyond the doorway to make sure to not be the first one out. Once he saw that other recruits had begun to trickle out, he joined them by standing outside his door. A look of panic was still planted on his face. His heart continued to thump.

"Eleveners, follow me!" a Commander called out from the end of the hallway. Kain turned to his right and saw a young boy with short, shaggy black hair standing in front of the next door over from his. The boy was looking at Kain curiously. Kain's eyes fluttered nervously as he followed the Commander through the hall. The boy walked up beside Kain.

"Are you really Victor Villairo's son?" the boy asked. He had a playful innocence about him. He was slightly smaller than the other eleven-year-olds, but he didn't look weak. Kain glanced over and shrugged before looking back at the ground.

"Yeah, I am." Kain answered quietly. The boy raised his eyebrows. He was smiling with his mouth wide open. "I didn't know him though. He died before I was even born."

"Wow." Demitri said under his breath. Kain looked down at his feet. "I'm Demitri." The boy stuck out his arm. Kain whipped his head over and stared at the open hand. He slowly reached his arm out and shook Demitri's hand.

"I'm Kain."

Demitri nodded as he answered, "I know."

The boys soon reached a series of massive circular buildings where each age group was respectively led into. The mob of eleven-year-olds cautiously filtered through the wide-open double doors and into the room. Sand covered the floor inside of the brick structure. A circle marked in red paint was laid out near the center of the room. The boys came up and stood around it, anxiously waiting for their instructor to address them.

At this time, the King and Drake had just reached the training facility complex across the city. Drake then raised his hand to his forehead and looked over to the King before saying, "Oh, my Lord, I nearly forgot. There are whispers that a boy we picked up from Valgard is the son of Victor Villairo. But, surely this can't be possible, right? Wouldn't the Kingdom know if he had fathered any offspring?" The King pursed his lips and again tilted his head.

"How old is this boy?" King Alastor asked while he chewed on his fingernails.

"I believe he's eleven, sir." Drake responded, rubbing the back of his neck.

King Alastor came to a halt; then he turned to Drake and smiled. "Well then, let's go see the Eleveners and find out." Alastor ordered.

The King and his Hand entered the training room of the Eleveners just as the Commander was beginning to explain the game to the boys. The sight of the King and Drake stopped him in his tracks, but Alastor waved for him to continue along with his instruction.

The Commander turned his attention back to the crowd of boys and continued, "As I was saying, you will all be fighting today. One on one. Winner stays, loser, well … don't lose. Now who wants to start us off?" A boy with short, blond hair shot out from the crowd. He stepped into the circle and began twirling his wooden sword. He skipped around with a bold show of confidence. The instructor clapped his hands together and grinned. "Alright then! And who is to be the challenger?" The mob of boys stood still and silent. "Don't make me choose!"

The King watched the crowd patiently. The boys remained frozen in fear as the passing silence became unbearably awkward.

"Isn't that supposed to be Victor Villairo's kid? Make him go!" one boy in the crowd whispered. Kain looked over at Demitri with his eyes wide open. The murmurs soon became louder and louder until eventually hands started pushing at Kain. After a few seconds, he was launched out from the herd and into the circle. Kain stumbled forward; once he regained his balance, he looked up at the Commander.

"It appears we have our challenger!" the loud voice bellowed. The Commander grabbed the kids by their chest plates and brought them closer to the center of the circle. Kain's blood ran cold. He was frozen. He gulped as the boy in front of him menacingly eyed him while pacing back and forth. Kain held his sword in his right hand and crouched over slightly, trembling uncontrollably. "First one to step out of the circle loses. Anything and everything is allowed, but to win, you must get the other one out of the circle," the Commander explained. He watched the two boys intently as he placed his hand between them. "Ready … go!"

The boy immediately came darting toward Kain. Kain managed to dodge the first few swings but ended up taking a hard hit on his shoulder. All his training seemed to vanish as he was now acting purely on instinct. After not being able to get a single swing off and taking quite the beating, Kain tripped and fell just beside the line of the circle. The boy backed away, strutting around the remaining open space.

Kain knew he had to get up; there wasn't another choice. He took a deep breath, rose and tried to engage, but the boy came even faster this time. Kain lost his footing, flailed his sword and took a hard swing to the head. He was knocked out briefly on his fall to the ground. He opened his eyes as he laid on the floor. Tears began to well in his eyes as he clenched his jaw. His head was throbbing. He looked up and saw the same smug expression on the boy's face.

Kain smacked his fist on the ground, gripped his sword and shot up. His opponent's facial expression shifted from smug to surprised. Kain readied himself and took a deep breath. As he looked at the boy's devious face, he felt a white-hot rage begin to swell within him. He was no longer afraid, but angry. He hated the boy. Kain assumed a fighting stance. The boy immediately stepped toward him and swung for his head. Kain ducked, came up and connected with a two-handed swing to the boy's rib cage.

The boy backed away, wincing in pain. He then struck back at Kain, yelling out in frustration. This time, Kain took him on. Their wooden swords met. They continued to clash back and forth until the boy tried to take a slice downward at Kain's shoulder. Kain sidestepped, leaving the boy completely exposed. Kain took advantage of the opening and struck at the boy's head. The strike landed and the boy was sent tumbling down just beside the circle line.

The boy got up, now dazed and certainly less confident than before. He tried his best to reposition himself, but he was injured, and he knew it. Kain took the offensive and came rushing forward, lashing his sword back and forth at both sides of the boy. After a flurry of swings, the young boys eventually managed to get their swords to lock. They momentarily remained stalled together as they locked eyes and pressed hard against each other. Kain disengaged and spun, swinging for the boy's head. The wooden blade connected with the back of the boy's skull and sent him crashing down toward Kain. During the fall, Kain yanked his left knee up and knocked the boy right in the mouth. Once his head hit Kain's knee, the boy was sent hurling backwards where he ultimately landed just outside the paint line. His face was smeared red with the blood pouring out from his nose. His body was sprawled across the sandy floor, completely unconscious.

Kain now walked the circle with a sense of confidence he had never felt before. He looked at the boy on the ground; then he looked back at the crowd. His face had hardened; he no longer felt panic. Only anger surged through him now.

"Who's next then?" Kain yelled. The crowd stayed silent as they looked at the boy who was now spitting up blood and writhing in pain on the ground. Kain glared at him coldly; then he looked back at the crowd. He twirled his sword and regained a fighting stance.

"Well, doesn't he look just like his father?" the King whispered through a smile.

PART II

CHAPTER 5

"**G**od damn it! I said to keep them alive!" Drake called out as he sprinted through the sand to catch up with Kain.

Kain turned around and threw his hands up. "But they were getting away!" He protested.

Drake yelled back, "And we would have caught them! We're out in the desert. Not very many places to hide, are there?" Drake rushed up to Kain and scowled at him with his arms folded. "King Alastor explicitly wanted them alive. You're going to be the one who answers for this." Drake glared at his student with squinted eyes. "I should've never taught you how to throw those daggers. You can't help yourself with them." Kain rolled his eyes and looked back at the other boys. He rubbed his chin which had begun to sprout a few dark hairs.

Kain then shook his head and yelled, "Come on guys! You all saw them! Back me up! What was I supposed to do?" The crowd of boys stood there silently, looking back and forth between Kain and Drake. Kain sighed and slouched his shoulders. Drake crept over and inspected the two dead bodies. He bit the side of his check and then looked back at the group of boys.

"Well, help me carry them at least," Drake ordered. He grunted as he knelt down and pulled the daggers out of their backs. Kain stood by awkwardly as a few of the boys came forward to help Drake pick them up. Drake gazed out at the sandy hills that surrounded them and explained, "Getting these guys back to the boat is going to be tough; we should probably stick them on a horse and walk beside it. It'll slow us down, but King Alastor is going to want proof they're dead."

"Can't we just take their heads?" Kain offered. Drake came to a halt, staring at Kain curiously. He then dropped the dead man from his shoulder.

"Alright Kain, take their heads then." Kain paused when Drake gave his instruction.

"I … uh." Kain was flustered. His hands trembled slightly as he looked down at the bodies. He had killed many times, but he hadn't done anything quite as gruesomely intimate as this. After a long silence, Drake walked up to him and leaned over, narrowing his eyes as he pressed his finger into Kain's chest.

"Well? Someone's gotta take their heads off, and you had the idea. Are you really going to make one of these other boys do it?" Drake asked while he bent over. His eyes were locked with Kain's. His brutish and square face was now within just a few inches of Kain's.

Kain knew he couldn't place the burden of taking the dead men's heads on another one of the boys. He had to be the one to do it. He reached behind his back and slowly pulled out his sword. He cautiously approached the two bodies as his heart started to thump. After taking a deep breath, he raised his sword and cut down hard. Blood spattered all over him as the head of the first man rolled aside. Kain let out a deep breath and relaxed.

"Well that wasn't so bad," Kain said as he regained his composure and walked over to the next corpse. He wound up and struck downward. The head split from its body, rolled and bumped into the other skull where it came to a halt. Kain leaned over and turned his head to the group of boys behind him. He stuck his arm out. "Someone hand me a couple of towels." One of the boys tossed Kain two white rags. Kain wrapped the heads in the cloth and then glanced up at Drake.

"Very good. You're gonna need to be getting used to that. Now— " Drake was cut off as arrows suddenly began to zip past them. He immediately turned to see what was coming for them. "Boys! Take cover!" The group of young men looked around desperately for something to shield them from the assault. They scattered and took refuge behind the boulders littered throughout the desert hills.

A few enemy men were now running out from the small caves in the distance, charging toward the boys and Drake. Each loaded his bow with another arrow and shot. They were only about fifty yards away at this point. Drake started running to cover, but before he reached the nearest boulder, he was struck in the calf muscle by an arrow. He screamed and reached for his leg.

"Boys! Get back to the ship! Get out of here!" Drake commanded as he stumbled to the ground and crashed into the sand.

Kain stuck his head up from behind a boulder and looked down at Drake and then at the men making their way toward them. He ran forward, scooped up the two heads of the dead men and then ran in the opposite direction of the assailants. The six boys gathered next to their tied-up horses and mounted them. Once they were all on, they bolted up and over the hills in search of safety.

As soon as the boys had gotten over a few of the hills and out of sight, Kain called out to them, "Hey, stop here!" They slowed and circled around each other. "We can't leave Drake. We have to go back for him. He'd never leave us behind."

"What's your plan then? We can't take on grown men with just the six of us." Demitri challenged. Kain looked over at him. Demitri was anxiously scratching his shaved head.

"First of all, yes we absolutely can," Kain stated. He then turned around to face the other boys. "We just have to first figure out where they're taking him. I think those men who attacked us are from Cophina. Drake was telling me on the boat ride over that the town sits at the base of a canyon. It apparently has only one real access point; then the perimeter becomes completely enveloped by the canyon walls. That's where Drake thought the defectors were headed. Drake was worried that if they took refuge there we would have essentially no chance at capturing them because of the town's geography." Kain faced the direction they had arrived from. "But you all stay here; I'll figure out if that's in fact where our attackers are headed, and then I'll come back with all of the information that I can gather." The boys were scared. They had never been abroad without a Commander. Even still, they chose to put their trust in Kain.

"How do you know Drake will still be alive by the time you get back?" Demitri asked.

Kain gave a half smile before responding, "He's the Royal Hand of Nymea. They're going to want to interrogate him for a while if and before they execute him. We'll have at least a few hours, especially knowing Drake. He's a pro." Kain licked his lips and grinned. The boys nodded back at him.

Kain loaded up one of the horses and started to carefully make his way back to where they had been attacked. He tied his horse to a small tree branch shortly before he reached the crest of the hill overlooking the valley where they had been fired upon. He crept up and peeked over. He could see Drake, now shackled and being forced to walk behind his captors with the arrow still sticking out of his calf. He limped along as he was dragged by a rope.

For the next half an hour, Kain carefully tracked the men through the desert back to their village. Drake had been correct in his initial description of the village's geography. Cophina did sit in the cove of a small canyon. The opening to the village was bottlenecked, allowing for only one way in and out of the town. But on both sides of the small inlet to the village, the steep canyon facades began to rise, fortifying the town's perimeter in a circle of canyon walls nearly fifty feet tall. The village itself was tucked against the back of the cove.

Kain discreetly made his way to the top of the canyon's edge and scoped out the village carefully. He got on his stomach and inspected the layout of the town. He saw that the entrance into the village immediately led to the town square, and at the center sat the gallows which also faced outward to the village entrance. It was a straight shot from the gallows to the exit of the town. Kain did one last scan of the village and then snuck back to his horse. He hopped up on its back and returned to the group of boys waiting for him.

When Kain arrived, the boys surrounded him. Demitri cocked his head to the side as he asked, "Well, do you have a plan?"

Kain nodded, rubbed his chin for a few moments and then replied, "I think so. Does anyone know exactly what we have in terms of weaponry?"

One of the boys spoke up, "Well, we have four horses obviously, but all our actual weapons are on the ship. The only things we have on us are our swords."

"I know all that. I want to know what we have onboard." Kain said impatiently as he looked around at the boys.

"We have a ton of bows and arrows, spears; I brought some of my throwing knives. Pretty much everything. King Alastor gave us the standard arsenal," Demitri said, not exactly sure what Kain was getting at.

Kain gazed around at the boys now with a slight smile on his face. He clapped his hands together and explained, "Well alright then. I think I do have a plan. We only have a couple of hours from now to get this right though. You all need to go back to the ship as fast as you can. Gather as many arrows as your sheaths can hold. Bring four bows. Grab your knives Demitri. Get two spears and two cloaks. Demitri and Alexei, you're the two best spear throwers, and you're going to need to be deadly accurate today. The rest of you, I hope you had a lot of bow practice at the academy." Kain finished telling the boys the plan and then sent them off to return to their ship docked along the coastline.

Before they headed back to the coast on horseback, one of the boys asked, "Won't you be needing a horse Kain?"

"Nope. You guys are going to need all the horses. Plus, I need to be inconspicuous," Kain called back while he looked over his shoulder and smiled at them. "For now, at least." He took off on foot toward Cophina.

CHAPTER 6

Drake was now being taken out of the town prison and led up to the gallows. His face was stained with dirt and blood. His shackles were being pulled by the rope attached to them and he was being yanked up toward the wooden platform while a small group of soldiers escorted him. After walking up the stairs of the gallows, Drake leaned back against the wall behind him and faced the noose that was now directly in front of him. As he stared at the rope, he noticed a few soldiers pulling another prisoner out in the distance.

"Kain! I told you to get back to the ship!" Drake screamed from atop the platform.

"Well, it's not like I was going to just leave you!" Kain shouted back as he was now being dragged toward the gallows. Drake shook his head in frustration.

"God damn it," Drake whispered while still glaring at Kain.

One of the soldiers escorting Kain up to his execution called out to his Commander, "Sir, we found this one lurking around the archive room. We noticed the Nymean Lion crest on his chest plate and brought him in at once. He was unarmed." The Commander standing beside Drake on the platform nodded once the soldier relayed the information to him.

"Bring him up here, and get another noose," the Commander ordered. The soldier nodded, he then tugged at Kain and pulled him forward. Kain looked up and scanned the top of the canyon. The sun's evening rays were now beginning to shine right over the top of the walls. A massive shadow now covered the town. Kain could barely see the heads of the boys popping out from atop the canyon walls.

"Great. Now we're both dead," Drake whispered as soon as Kain was brought up beside him.

"Don't worry." Kain reassured Drake. He had a big smile on his face. "I've got a plan." Drake and Kain were now standing side by side in shackles and eyeing the nooses in front of them.

"Where's Demitri and the others?" Drake asked under his breath.

"Now you're getting the idea." Kain replied. Drake rolled his eyes and shook his head. "This better fucking work kid."

Kain stood smiling as he confidently glanced over at Drake. The Commander was now making his way over to them through the crowd of villagers below. The man stomped his way up the steps to the gallows. His oversized and flashy armor clanked as he marched across the wooden platform. He glared at Kain and Drake the entire time.

The Commander began to speak in a gravelly voice, "You've both been identified as spies of Nymea. If you want quick deaths, you'll tell me what brought you here to Cophina."

"Well sir … the thing is, I don't know that I actually want a quick death," Kain taunted. Drake growled and looked over at him. The Commander punched Kain in the stomach. Kain hunched over and let out a soft moan.

"You're gonna regret that one," Kain choked out as he glared up at the Commander.

"Is that so boy?" the Commander asked, slightly amused. Kain rose back up and met his eyeline. "Forget the nooses. Bring me the scythe!" The Commander turned and walked off the platform.

Kain leaned to his right and whispered to Drake, "When I tell you, put your hands up over your head and against the wall behind us." Drake gave a slight nod.

The Commander came back up on the platform with a scythe in hand. He nearly pressed his nose against Kain's while giving a sneering smile.

"You're gonna get cut up real nice boy." The Commander said as he touched the blade of his scythe.

Kain stared the Commander down, then looked out into the crowd, nodded and yelled, "Now!"

Kain and Drake launched their hands above their heads as two spears cut through the air. The spears broke apart the chains between Kain and Drake's hands and were now stuck against the wall behind them. Kain used his freed hands to yank the spear above him out. He spun it around and shoved it through the Commander's stomach. Kain pulled the spear out of the man's gut and swiped it across his face, knocking the Commander off the platform. Kain looked to his left and saw a soldier climbing the stairs to meet him. Kain butted the soldier in the head with his spear, flipped it around and then stabbed him in the chest and left the spear stuck in him.

Drake had removed his spear from the wall and proceeded to take on one of the men coming up the stairs on the other side of the platform. Arrows were now flying from the top of the canyon. They rained down, striking the enemy soldiers occupying the perimeter of the crowd. Suddenly, two hooded figures on horses came storming through the mob of villagers and rode right up next to the wooden platform.

"Let's go!" Kain yelled out as he and Drake leapt from the platform and onto the backs of the horses. "Ride!" They burst through the crowd of citizens and rode straight for the canyon outlet. The other boys took off from the top of the canyon and were now heading away from the town and toward the coast. A squadron of enemy soldiers hopped onto horses and chased after them. Kain looked back behind him and saw the relatively large group of soldiers now on their tail.

Kain called out, "Demitri! Hand me your knives!" Demitri reached into his cloak, pulled out a pouch and handed it to Kain. "Alright, now hold me steady!" Kain flipped around on the horse. He and Demitri were now sitting back-to-back while Demitiri rode forward. Demitri stuck his arm behind him and held onto the back of Kain's chest plate collar. Kain unfolded the pouch of knives.

"Are you sure you got this Kain?" Drake shouted. Kain looked to his left and nodded.

"Here we go," Kain whispered through a smile. He reached his arm up and sent one of the knives flying. It pinned the targeted soldier in the face and sent him tumbling from his horse. Drake glanced over at Kain, impressed by the precision of the throw.

"Nice one Kain!" Demitri howled. Kain took a deep breath and pulled another knife from the pouch. He cocked his arm back and sent the knife soaring through the air. It struck its target and took yet another soldier off their tail.

"One more should scare them off for good," Drake said as Kain nodded in agreement. Kain then took aim once again. Bullseye. A third soldier was hit in the chest and fell off his horse and onto the ground. The additional men in the pack following them began to slow their horses and turn around.

The four boys that Kain had perched on top of the canyon had now caught up with Kain, Drake, Alexei and Demitri. The rough and blue waters of the Aspero Ocean were finally in their sight. They grouped up and stormed toward the beach.

"Great fucking aim Kain!" one of the boys called out as they all came together. Kain smiled with pride as he flipped around.

"Sorry about your knives Demitri!" Kain apologized.

"Are you kidding? That was awesome. Show me how to do that back at the Capital!"

The group of boys had finally reached the sandy beaches of the desert island. Their ship sat docked along the water's edge. They slowed their horses and jumped to the ground. Kain and Drake dismounted. Kain glanced up at Drake.

"Well, didn't do too bad of a job saving you, huh?" Kain joked. Drake stared back at him. He was frustrated with Kain's disobedience and yet couldn't help but feel a great deal of pride in his protege.

"That was pretty damn impressive, kid. But will you do what I say next time please?" Drake replied. He then folded his massive arms and shook his head slightly. Kain looked at Drake proudly before pulling the saddle off his horse.

Kain explained, "You know if I had you'd probably be dead by now, right?"

Drake continued to shake his head, he answered, "Actually, I can take care of myself." He patted Kain on the back as Kain gave a joyful smile. "Come on, let's get on the boat and get the hell out of here."

CHAPTER 7

After reaching the shores of Nymea, Drake and the boys docked their ship and rode their horses for the next few hours back to the Capital. Upon their arrival in the city, one of the King's aides told them that they were wanted in the throne room as soon as possible. They set their things down, climbed the stairs and then made their way through the grand entrance into the palace.

Once Drake and the boys had walked through the doors, they followed the red carpet that led up to the King's throne. They stopped shortly before reaching the base of the staircase that the throne sat atop. King Alastor rose from his seat and spread his arms out wide, welcoming them with a smile.

"Ah, it is good to see that you all returned safely. Now, tell me what occurred," the King said as he then sat down, crossed his legs and folded his arms. "Where are the prisoners?" His tone was now much more serious.

Kain dropped the heads of the two men on the ground and then spoke up, "Your majesty, they were … about to escape. I had to resort to using lethal force, unfortunately." Kain wouldn't meet the King's gaze. Alastor sat in silence for a few moments, inspecting the heads of the dead men while he tapped his fingers on his knee.

King Alastor scowled then explained, "Well … that would make the mission a failure then. These men were defectors of the crown. I needed to know why, and what their plans were. The mission was to bring them back to me alive, Kain." Kain looked up nervously at Alastor who now appeared to be on the brink of a rage-induced tirade.

Drake stepped forward and interrupted, "To be fair, my Lord, I must say, Kain was the real hero of the mission." Alastor tilted his head and stared at Drake. "He is correct; the men were getting away and likely heading back to Cophina. If they had reached the town, I'm not sure we would have even been able to kill them, let alone capture them. Not only that, but immediately after Kain had managed to kill the men, I myself was taken hostage after being shot in the leg and essentially immobilized. I told the boys to get to the ship, leave me for dead and return to the Capital. Well, Kain disobeyed. He came up with a plan to save me instead. And I have to admit I have never seen such military prowess from a seventeen-year-old. It was really something, your majesty." Kain glanced over at Drake with a slight smile, he then quickly turned away and fluttered his eyes to the ground. "He allowed himself to be captured, brought to hang alongside me, antagonized their Commander, and then positioned these boys perfectly to get us out. Not only did Kain make the best of a very difficult situation, but he certainly saved my life, and with a great deal of risk to his own. If the blame of failure is being handed out, I deserve it, my Lord. Not Kain."

Alastor sat back with his hand on his chin; he was looking over at Kain when he replied, "That is indeed very impressive Kain. It seems this mission perhaps should have been planned better from the start. No punishment shall be given for this matter. At least the two traitors have been killed." King Alastor looked around at the other boys. "Now, why don't you all freshen up and when you've finished, return to the banquet hall for a special dinner. We have visitors from the Galgarian Kingdom here, and it is essential that our relationship be reconciled if we are to avoid a war." Drake and the boys bowed and walked away.

After quickly washing, Kain shook out his wet, long and curly brown hair, put his jet-black armor back on, sheathed his sword on his back and headed out of his barrack. Kain and the rest of the boys grouped up together outside of their rooms and walked over to the banquet hall. Demitri and Kain led the pack as they passed through the corridors beneath the palace.

Demitri looked over his shoulder at Kain and said, "For a second there, I thought you might have been in some serious trouble with King Alastor."

Kain raised his eyebrows and glanced down at the cobblestone floor before replying, "Yeah, that was quite the praise by Sir Drake. I thought I was going to get the whip again until he stepped in." Kain reached behind him and rubbed the top of his back.

"Do you know anything more about the two defectors? What brought them to Cophina and what they were looking for?" Demitri asked.

Kain shook his head and answered, "I know King Alastor suspected they were working for the Galgarians. But I'm not sure what could have brought them all the way out to the Barain Islands. Whatever the case, hopefully this banquet will help ease the tension along the eastern border. I'm not sure how long we can remain at this stalemate and not have conflict erupt. It's been years now. But … it does sound like the Galgarians are willing to try for peace. I guess we'll have to see."

The boys headed through the underground hallways until finally reaching a staircase. They made their way up the spiral staircase and found themselves at the back entrance of the banquet hall. One by one they slipped through the back door. The dinner had already begun, and the city nobles were dancing and eating all throughout the hall. The royal band played their harps and violins as servers sped in and out of the hall, bringing more food and removing empty plates.

King Alastor was seated at a long table that lined nearly the full length of one of the walls. To his left and his right sat a Galgarian emissary along with a Galgarian security man. Alastor was excitedly whispering to the emissary who wore a long, white robe with green trim along the collar. His head was bald, and his skin was quite pale. He was smiling slightly and nodding every few seconds while he stared forward.

Kain scanned the room before looking over curiously at the security man beside Alastor. The man had long and greasy black hair that hung over his face, but beneath it rested a sinister expression. His eyes kept fluttering around the room and then back to his food. He chewed at his chicken leg ferociously, looking tense the entire time.

Kain approached the buffet table and filled a plate. He then crept over to a huddle of boys that had formed in the corner.

"Does something seem off to you all about the Galgarian security man? He looks incredibly on edge." Kain asked the group around him. The boys then looked over and inspected the man.

"I mean, he is security; it would make sense that he's constantly on edge, looking out for danger," one of the boys said.

Kain kept his gaze stuck on the security man while he responded, "Yeah, but I don't know. I'm not sensing the typical caution that you'd expect. He seems to be up to something … but worried about getting caught. Or perhaps *noticed*, even." Kain turned back to the boys. "Maybe it's nothing," he added as he bit into his food.

In another corner of the banquet hall, a separate group of young cadets had huddled together. They were eyeing Kain and his friends.

One of the boys spoke up, "Did you all hear about Kain Villairo's mission? I heard he killed twenty men himself, broke into the city center of Cophina and freed Sir Drake single-handedly. He even killed the two defectors and took their heads back with him." The boy's mouth was wide open as he looked over at Kain. One of the other boys in the group with straight, long, blond hair, tan skin and soft but menacing features glanced over bitterly at the boy who had just spoken.

The blond boy then responded in a sharp tone, "Yes, yes, Kain Villairo. The savior of Nymea. Nonsense. That couldn't have been what happened. He's a mere Junior Knight. I swear I'll never understand the King's fondness for him. He's a fraud, like his traitor father before him." The boy sneered and stared at Kain with disgust. "He's nothing special."

"Are you sure you're not just jealous that Sir Drake didn't pick you for the mission, Ivan?" the other boy asked.

Ivan launched his hand swiftly at the boy's throat and whispered through clenched teeth, "It'd be wise for you to keep your stupid questions to yourself." The boy backed away and pushed Ivan's arm off of himself. Ivan relaxed and stepped back, still keeping his gaze fixated on Kain. Ivan crossed his arms. "We'll see in time what type of soldier he is. And where his loyalties lie. I just hope the King can see through it early enough."

King Alastor rose from his table and rang the bell beside him, gathering the attention of all the partygoers throughout the hall. The music halted and everyone turned their eyes toward the King. He opened his arms and gave an insincere smile that showed his mangled and yellow teeth. His blood red robes hung loosely over his body.

The King announced, "I hope you are enjoying the party! As usual, eat and drink as much as your stomachs will allow. Tonight, we are graced with the presence of the Galgarian Kingdom's royal emissary, as well as his security man." Alastor looked to both his left and right. The emissary calmly nodded and smiled. The security man continued looking anxious while he scanned every corner of the room. The King continued, "We are discussing cordial means to end this territorial dispute along the eastern border. With the graciousness of these fine men, I feel we will indeed reach a solution soon. So by all means, this calls for a celebration!" The crowd cheered as the

King sat and continued his conversation.

After another hour of music and dance, Kain had made his way back to the buffet table, which was stationed a few feet from where the King sat. The King took notice and waved Kain over to him. Kain approached the table and bowed before Alastor and the two Galgarians.

The King turned to the two men and said, "Medax, Dolofinus, this here is Kain Villairo. He is our most promising young soldier." Kain nodded.

"Thank you, my Lord. Pleasure to meet you both." Kain responded, looking back and forth between the two men. The emissary smiled and nodded. The security man glared at Kain with a grimacing stare. Kain cocked his head to the side and returned an equally menacing gaze.

The King turned his head and looked down across the table and called out, "Sir Drake, come, join us. Let us take a walk in the courtyard." Drake nodded, wiped the food off his face and rose from his seat. They all gathered together and headed outside. The royal guards began to follow, but Alastor turned and waved them off.

"We are amongst friends here," Alastor said in a warm tone. He then smiled at the emissary as they left the banquet hall and headed out into the courtyard. The moonlight's shine and the torches along the walls illuminated their walk through the garden. The stars had lit the night sky's shade into a beautiful purple haze. The sky glimmered above them while they strolled alongside King Alastor.

The King spoke, "It has been, discouraging, seeing such tensions along the border continue to persist. I feel now that with you understanding my side, and I yours, a meeting between King Timios and I may finally bear fruit." The emissary nodded in agreement.

Kain was on the far-left side of the group, right beside the security man who was walking next to the King. They came upon the balcony of the courtyard and Alastor leaned against the guardrail. Kain, Drake and the emissary did the same. The men stared out at the night sky, taking in the beauty of the forest beneath them. The Casgardian

Mountains in the distance cut along the horizon line where they met the sea of stars above. The men stood in silence.

Kain then glanced to his right. He noticed the security man hadn't approached the railing. He was standing a few feet back behind Alastor with his left hand curled and tucked tightly at his side. Kain pivoted his right foot back and steadied his hand.

The security man then scrunched his face angrily and yanked his left arm up. Kain pulled his sword from his back and swung upwards at the man's arm, slicing it clean off. Alastor instantly spun around while Drake restrained the emissary.

The security man fell to his knees screaming as blood gushed from his arm. He gripped his shoulder and growled. He glared up at King Alastor who was now looking down at the man with fire in his eyes. Alastor's face had gone cold; his nostrils flared as fury radiated from him. Kain held his sword down with the point pressed firmly against the man's neck. The emissary was silent while Drake restrained his arms.

"Now I see what this has been about," the King snapped. He slowly turned his head to face the emissary. "You thought you could come here to kill me? The Galgarian Kingdom will face the full force and fury of the entire Nymean Empire. I will not rest until I have exterminated every single one of your wretched men. And that is a promise I do not make lightly." Alastor got within inches of the man's face and gnashed his teeth. The emissary scowled at the King as he shifted his arms. Drake squeezed him tight.

"Should I kill him, my Lord?" Drake asked as he glared at the back of the emissary's head.

The King looked back and forth between the two Galgarians and ordered, "Not yet. Take them to the dungeon. If this one here even makes it down there alive, we will soon find out what they know." He glanced down at the assassin. Blood gushed out of him.

"If you kill me, you yourself will face the wrath of the Galgarians! You think you can continue to take our land from us? I can assure you this war will not be won without devastation to all!" the emissary yelled while Drake pulled him away. Kain held his sword to the assassin's neck and led him down to the dungeon alongside Drake.

CHAPTER 8

Kain was lying in bed later that night when he heard harsh pounding on his door. He got up and put on his robes. When he unlatched his lock, a royal guard was standing outside his door.

"The King requests your presence in the throne room." There was a metallic ring to the guard's voice that creeped Kain out.

Once the guard relayed the message, he immediately marched away. Kain peeked his head out of the door before walking down the hallway toward the throne room. When he made it up the steps of the balcony, he pushed open the massive doors to the throne room and saw Alastor and Drake in the middle of a heated conversation.

"He's not ready, my Lord!" Drake pleaded with King Alastor. "How will the men that are twice his age view it? He's too stubborn. He needs more time."

Kain awkwardly tiptoed up the red carpet. When Alastor and Drake glanced up and noticed him, they stopped talking. Both stared at him. The King gave a pleasant smile and waved him toward them. Kain paced forward along the red carpet and eventually reached the base of the stairs that led up to the throne. Drake stood on the second step looking down at Kain with a worried expression on his face.

"Kain Villairo." Alastor smiled warmly as he addressed Kain. "Ever since you arrived here, I have seen with my own eyes the many gifts you have been granted. They rival those of even the greatest warriors throughout history. The countless hours of training, successful missions, along with the initiative you took to save Sir Drake in the Barain Islands, as well as the courage, instinct and ability you showed when you saved my life this evening have brought me to a realization." The King paused and briefly glanced over at Drake. "As we begin this war with the Galgarians, I want you to help lead us to victory. I hereby promote you in rank, from Junior Knight, to Commander." Drake looked displeased, but he didn't dare say anything. He shook his head and bit his fingernails.

Kain's eyes opened wide as he blurted out, "A Commander? Me? But, I haven't even reached Knighthood yet. Are you sure?" The King rose from his throne and walked down the steps. He put his hand on Kain's shoulder.

"You will be the youngest Commander in Nymean history my boy," the King declared. Kain gulped, furrowed his brow and nodded.

"I—I won't let you down, your majesty." Kain promised, he then looked up at Alastor.

"I know you won't." The King said as he patted Kain on the shoulder. "Now, kneel before me." Kain dropped down and the King placed his sword upon Kain's shoulders. "Rise my friend." Kain stood while trying to hold back his smile. "We will be sending the first regiment of our army to Fort Malum at daybreak to meet the Galgarian forces. Sir Drake will show you the brigade of men you will be commanding." Kain stared at the King, still in disbelief. His mind was racing. "Prepare yourself my boy, for the drums of war do not ever beat lightly." Kain nodded fiercely and left the hall.

As soon as Kain had exited the doors, Alastor turned back to Drake and gave his command, "Sir Drake, send a legion of men out to the villages to increase resource production. We will need all that we can get." Drake nodded. "At dawn, ride to Fort Malum with brigades one through six and meet up with General Archie and our regiment currently stationed on the Tenebris River. The fort sits just across the water from the Galgarian city of Arcem. Kain will command the first brigade. We won't be using the full force of our military yet. We need to get a feel for them, their power, and what they're willing to do. But Drake." Alastor then stared at Drake with his cold, dead eyes. "I do intend to kill every last one of them. No matter what it takes. No matter how long it takes."

"Yes, your majesty." Drake whispered. He then bowed and walked away.

The next morning Kain geared up for battle. He stood in front of his mirror as he removed his chest plate from the wooden rack it hung from. He placed the chest plate over his head and strapped it tight. The Nymean Lion crest sat proudly etched into his armor beneath a layer of black leather.

Kain then slipped on his arm and shin guards before lacing up his boots. Finally, he took his sword off his mantle and slowly sheathed it onto his back. He stared at himself in the mirror, tucked his hair behind his ears and pounded his chest. He took off for the city square.

When Kain arrived at the square, he saw the six brigades lined up in boxed formations. Drake and the four other Commanders were conversing in a huddle at the front of the armies. As Kain approached, none of them even turned their heads. All were at least twenty-five years old.

Once Drake noticed Kain, he cut in, "Men. This is Kain Villairo, Commander of the first brigade." The four Commanders instantly turned and stared at Kain with emotionless faces. They didn't say a word. Kain looked around at them, unsure of how to react.

Kain then nodded and addressed the men, "Pleasure to fight beside each of you." The men ignored his comment and turned back to their huddle, continuing their conversation.

Drake stepped away, grabbed Kain by the arm, took him aside and said in a hushed tone, "Listen kid, this isn't going to be easy for you. I told King Alastor I didn't think you were ready. That's not a knock on you either. But you're seventeen. Some of the men in your brigade are nearly thirty. Commanding their respect isn't going to come easy, and getting the respect of the Commanders is going to be virtually impossible. Look, I'm on your side here, but this is going to be a real challenge. Are you sure you can handle it?" Kain looked forward for a moment without saying anything.

Kain then replied, "I know it won't be easy. I know I'm young. But I also know that I can do this. I want to do this." Kain turned his head and stared up at Drake. His mentor nodded and patted him on the back.

"Alright then. Good luck. Now, when we start our march to Fort Malum, make sure to ride up front with us Commanders. We need to talk strategy. And I think we could use your help given that little plan you devised in Cophina." Kain nodded to Drake and jogged back to his group of soldiers.

The first brigade was lined up along the edge of the city square awaiting Kain's orders. As Kain looked over his sea of men, he spotted Demitri in the back corner and walked toward him. They both appeared jittery with excitement. Demitri stepped out of line and came up to meet him.

"Commander." Demitri said as he made a slightly sarcastic bow. Kain smiled and gave a nod. "I can't believe the King actually did it. You didn't even have to go through Knighthood!" Demitri hit Kain on the arm.

Kain shook his head and showed a half smile. He put his hands on his hips and looked up at the palace.

"Apparently I'm the youngest Commander in Nymea's history."

Kain told Demitri. "We'll see how it goes I guess."

Demitri patted Kain on the back and reassured him, "Well I'd follow you into battle any day, no matter how old you are." Kain shook his hand and headed over to the front of the army of men. He mounted his horse and began leading his men out of the city square. Ivan stood in the back of the second brigade, staring Kain down.

"I can't believe they made Villairo a Commander. What was King Alastor thinking?" Ivan hissed to himself.

The young soldier next to Ivan raised his eyebrows and gave his opinion, "I don't know, Ivan. Kain is easily the best fighter of anyone younger than twenty in the whole army. He really does have an exceptional military mind too. And not only did he rescue Sir Drake in the Barain Islands, but he even saved King Alastor from that assassination attempt. Not to mention, all in a matter of two days. If anyone deserves it, I think it's him. Besides, we need a young leader we can aspire to."

Ivan glared at the boy beside him and snapped, "Well you all just think he's so great. But I see through it." Ivan folded his arms as he stared at Kain across the hordes of soldiers. "He's the son of a traitor. It's in his very blood."

CHAPTER 9

After nearly a day of travel, the six brigades of the first regiment found themselves marching over the grassy hills that overlooked the walls of Fort Malum. The tips of the wooden beams that made up the edges of the fort had all been sharpened to a point. Three watchtowers popped up along the jagged perimeter of the structure. Soldiers were scanning the horizon from the tops of them. The gigantic fort sat right up against the strong, flowing waters of the Tenebris River with the edge of the forest running along the fort's northern border.

Kain, Drake and the other Commanders rode together up to the gates of Fort Malum while their soldiers followed behind. Shouts could be heard coming from the watchmen as the gates were promptly opened following their arrival. Men rushed outside to greet the regiment.

"Sir Drake! I received the King's pigeon. We're ready to fight alongside you," a soldier said frantically as he stood staring up at Drake. Drake towered over the man; a blank expression rested on his face while he stayed mounted on his horse.

"You got the message? It was addressed to General Archie. Where is he?" The concern in Drake's voice was obvious as it bellowed throughout the valley. The soldier shook his head and stared at the ground.

The soldier scratched his chin and answered, "General Archie has been missing since last night. He noticed some movement across the river and apparently went to investigate. No one has seen him since."

Drake squinted and looked across the water. Beyond the river was a grassy fairway nearly 300 feet wide, bordered by forests on each side. The field eventually led up to a stone castle that had only a single door allowing for entry. The walls of the castle were menacingly tall, with the front facade stretching across almost the entire pasture.

The soldier followed Drake's gaze and then informed him, "That's where the Galgarians are stationed. We haven't seen any movement from them in almost two days. That is, until General Archie supposedly noticed something. Regardless, we aren't sure what to make of it all."

Drake got down from his horse and walked over to the river's edge. He knelt down and stuck his hand into the cold and powerfully flowing water. The river didn't appear too deep, but it stretched across for nearly forty feet. While Drake stared out into the distance, the soldier crept up behind him.

"We haven't tried fording the river yet. It's been the line in the sand for both of our armies." the soldier explained.

Drake growled as he looked across the river at the Galgarian city of Arcem. The sun was nearly beneath the horizon behind them, and the shade of the trees completely enveloped them at this point in the evening. Drake stood and turned to the other Commanders.

"Get inside the fort; ready yourselves; prepare your brigades. We're laying siege on them tonight." When Drake gave the orders, Kain and the other men nodded. They rode through the doors and saw a massive number of soldiers spread out within the walls of Fort Malum.

Demitri came up to Kain once he saw him trickle in. "What's going on?" he asked.

Kain slid down from his horse, then answered, "Well, General Archie has been missing for a day now." Kain flashed a worried look to Demitri. "And I guess the Galgarians have been silent ever since they got word of the foiled assassination attempt. So, now Drake is saying he wants to capture the city tonight. But I'm not sure. It doesn't feel right. Their premature retreat seems unlikely. But I don't know what prompted their silence."

"Wow, tonight? That seems aggressive." Demitri said as he raised his eyebrows.

"Yeah, I'm supposed to get you guys into formation actually." Just as Kain said this, Drake yelled out to the soldiers inside the fort.

"Men! I've just been made aware of the situation regarding General Archie. This alleged capture along with the brazen assassination attempt by the Galgarians warrants our immediate military response. Ready yourselves and report to your Commander in half an hour. We will take the city tonight!" The men cheered ferociously before scurrying off to get ready for battle.

Not long after the order was given, soldiers began forming into their brigades around their respective Commander. They were fully ready for war. Kain was atop his horse looking out at his men. The excitement in the crowd was palpable. Drake rode up and down the front line inspecting the men before him.

"Soldiers! Move out!" Drake commanded.

The army stormed out of the front gate of Fort Malum and headed straight toward the Tenebris River. Once they had squeezed through the doors, the soldiers spread out along the edge of the water and awaited further instruction. Kain, Drake and the other Commanders were now sitting on their horses behind the hordes of men along the river's edge.

Drake yelled out the order to begin crossing the river. It was nearly dark now as the soldiers slowly tip-toed their way through the water. The deepest point of the river measured only around four feet, but the power and width of the waters really slowed the men down. Over the next ten minutes or so, the soldiers carefully made their way to the grassy fairway on the other side.

Kain scanned the area, searching for motion from enemy soldiers. The Galgarians had to have known by now that the King's army was fording the river. As soon as the infantrymen had crossed, Kain and the Commanders trudged along on horseback. Halfway through the river, Kain pulled his horse to a halt.

"Wait. Drake, this can't be right," Kain shouted as he yanked on his horse's collar. "No, it's a trap!"

Drake whipped his head back; his eyes widened as he looked at Kain. The other Commanders took no notice of Kain's warning.

"What do you mean? What's going on?" Drake yelled back.

Immediately after Kain called out to the men, the tiny door of the city at the end of the pasture burst open. A lone man with long, red hair braided down his back stepped outside and yelled a ghoulish howl. He wore thick arm guards and a bloody green vest. He raised his arm. In his hand he was holding the head of General Archie. The man then grimaced through his thick, red beard and tossed the head out onto the grass. The Royal Army yelled and began storming toward the city at the sight of their dead general. Kain sat back beside the river, zipping his head around trying to figure out what was going on.

Once the Royal Army had made some decent headway toward the front facade of the castle, the forest edges on each side of the royal soldiers began to rustle in the darkness. Shadowy figures flickered within the trees. Hordes of Galgarian soldiers then came bleeding out from the forest lines, swarming the much smaller Royal Army from both sides. The royal soldiers tried to reposition and prepare for the onslaught of men coming at them, but just as they managed to get into a decent formation, another wave of Galgarians started trickling out of the city walls to further surround them.

Kain rushed through the crowd on horseback and headed for the heart of the conflict. He ripped his sword from his back and sliced into a few of the Galgarians that had made their way into the center of the fight. He jumped from his stallion and started looking around for the men in his brigade. Rain began to pour down as enemy soldiers crashed into the Royal Army.

"First brigade! Retreat! We're outnumbered!" Kan ordered. A few soldiers looked back at him in confusion, but none began to retreat across the river. Kain shook his head as he looked around to see his men being senselessly cut down. He then turned and saw Ivan on top of a Galgarian, ruthlessly stabbing his sword into the enemy soldier.

"Ivan! Get the other men in your brigade! We have to retreat!" Kain pleaded.

Ivan pulled his sword from the corpse beneath him and whipped his head around. He glared at Kain. Ivan's face was stained with the dead Galgarian's blood.

"You're not my Commander," Ivan said as he leapt up and headed back into the action.

Kain rolled his eyes and started running around searching for Drake. Finding Drake was the only way Kain would be able to get enough men to actually listen to his retreat call. Kain ran through the battle, desperately looking throughout the crowd. Finally, he spotted Drake storming his way up to the castle wall.

Drake was steamrolling through men as he raced to confront General Archie's killer. Galgarians were bouncing off Drake as he lashed at anyone that got in his way. Soon enough he neared the castle wall. The Galgarian soldier looked out at the oncoming Drake and smiled. He jogged over to meet Drake.

A scowl remained planted on Drake's face. He yelled at the Galgarian, "Jarin!" Drake raised his sword and brought it straight down on the man. Jarin swung up and blocked the blow. Drake ripped his blade back and forth across his body while Jarin used his arm guards and sword to counter each strike.

Jarin smiled, showing rotting and yellow teeth. He ducked one of Drake's swings and stabbed at him. Drake flung his head back, watching as the sword came within inches of his head. Drake regained his balance and threw a two-handed swing across his body.

Jarin raised his left arm and caught the strike against his guard. He reached down and gripped Drake's forearm, and then sliced at Drake's neck with his sword in the other hand. Drake tumbled forward, breaking free from Jarin's grasp but falling in the process.

Drake rolled and stood back up. He paused for a moment, growled, and then brought his sword above his head and pounded on Jarin who stepped aside and took another swing for Drake's head. Drake tried to dodge, but Jarin's sword caught and sliced Drake's face from the corner of his mouth up to his ear. Drake hit the ground.

Kain watched as blood flew from the side of Drake's face. Kain's eyes opened wide as he sprinted even faster toward the two. Jarin stood over Drake while looking down and smiling at him. Jarin raised his short and pointed blade, getting ready to stab down. Kain yanked out his dagger and desperately threw it.

Jarin stumbled back and whipped his head up. Then he looked down at himself. The dagger had plunged into his right shoulder. He scanned the area around him while he pulled the knife out. Jarin soon spotted the oncoming Kain furiously sprinting toward him. Jarin threw the dagger aside and repositioned his sword, going in for the kill once more.

Kain leapt as far as he could; then he sliced his sword across his body as he fell toward Jarin and Drake. Kain's blade met with Jarin's, barely moving Jarin's stab away from Drake's body and diverting the sword off into the grass. Kain stared up at Jarin as he rested on Drake's unconscious body. Jarin glared back.

Kain disengaged, rolled off Drake and steadied himself. He carefully tried to draw Jarin away from Drake. Jarin took the bait and followed Kain into a more open patch of grass. Rain continued to soak the battlefield. Lightning began to crackle above them as the two stared each other down. Kain looked over to see Drake's bloody face.

Anger overtook Kain. He gripped his sword and lunged at Jarin. The two of them clashed instantly, holding their swords against each other. Kain scowled, punched Jarin in the face and then spun at him with his sword. Jarin was knocked off balance but regained it quickly enough to block the swing with his arm guard.

Kain backed off slowly, he then furiously began throwing strikes in every direction. Jarin stepped back and took the defensive. Jarin tossed aside every strike that came his way. After making no offensive progress, Kain stopped and dropped his sword to his side.

Jarin stepped back and knelt down. He picked up a shield from the ground and crossed it with his sword. Kain crept forward. Jarin swiped at Kain, but Kain backed away and narrowly dodged the strike.

Jarin came in full force at Kain, stabbing and swinging at him viciously. Kain ducked and dodged as fast as he could until finally Jarin's blade swept just above his head. Kain swung up and sliced Jarin across his tricep.

Jarin leapt back, looked at his arm and saw the blood trickle down. He snarled, wound up and threw his shield at Kain who quickly crossed his arms in front of his face, but the shield smacked against his left forearm, badly injuring him.

Kain stepped back as Jarin smiled. Kain dropped his injured left arm and raised his sword in his right hand. He turned sideways, put his right foot forward and stuck his sword out toward Jarin, baiting him to come in. Kain put all his weight on his right foot and kept his sword low.

Jarin charged, smacked Kain's sword down, and then came at him with a swing aimed directly for his neck. Kain fell to his knee, letting the swing slide just over the top of him. He then launched himself upwards. While Jarin was in close, Kain came up and knocked him in the side of the head with the butt of his hilt. Jarin was sent tumbling down, face first into the mud.

Kain flipped his blade in his hand and went in for the kill. As soon as Kain's sword came crashing down though, Jarin flipped over and threw a pile of mud that struck Kain in the eyes. Kain snapped his head back while Jarin jumped up and ran for the castle wall. Kain dropped his sword and rubbed the mud from his eyes. He faced the sky and let the downpouring rain wash the dirt from his eyes.

"Kain! Here!" a Commander who had been watching their fight rode up on horseback shouted. He tossed Kain a piece of cloth. Kain reached out and grabbed it. He wiped his eyes, tossed the rag aside and then looked up at the man. The Commander was in his late twenties. He had long, thick, black hair and a stern expression rested on his face. He looked down at Kain curiously.

"Commander Henry, we need to retreat if we want to have any semblance of an army left!" Kain screamed as he frantically looked around to see the devastating losses that the Royal Army had suffered. The Commander nodded his head slowly. Kain then rushed over to Drake who was still lying unconscious. Kain pressed on Drake's chest and looked up at Henry. "Get him out of here!" Kain called to a few nearby soldiers to pick Drake up off the ground and stick him onto the back of the Commander's horse. Henry nodded to Kain and then rushed toward the Tenebris River, yelling for the Royal Army to retreat. Men instantly turned away from the battle and headed back toward Fort Malum.

Kain was now sprinting as fast as he could, trying to break free from the gang of Galgarians following right on his heels. Once he reached the Tenebris River, he jumped as far as he could into the water. The rainfall had heightened the river and increased its flow speed significantly, and Kain struggled to get across as the current immediately swept him up. Thankfully, the Galgarians were not even trying to ford the river. Kain looked back and saw them standing along the edge, cheering in victory.

Halfway across the river, Kain saw a boulder poking out downstream. Kain tried to swim over to it. He was swept up by the current but managed to grab onto the rock at the last moment. He shut his eyes, laid his head on the boulder and took a deep breath. He then looked around and scanned the area, trying to see how the other men were handling the retreat. When he turned his head downstream, he saw Demitri barely staying afloat. His head bobbed up and down as he gasped for breath, trying to hold off the current.

Kain let go of the stone and floated down toward Demitri. The area he was in now was becoming more shallow. Kain planted his feet deep into the riverbed. The current dragged him, but his feet finally caught against the pebbles below him, almost bringing him to a full stop. He stretched out his hand while trying to stay balanced.

Demitri lunged for Kain's arm. As soon as he grabbed on, the current started pulling at them even harder. Kain couldn't stay planted where he was, so he kicked off and used the momentum to sway toward the other side of the river. Kain was treading water with one arm and carrying an exhausted Demitri in the other. The two were only five feet away from the river's edge, but they were quickly being swept downstream. When Kain glanced behind him, he saw that water was quickly falling from the edge of the river.

"Shit. Demitri!" Kain yelled, "We gotta get to shore! That waterfall will take us out!"

Demitri's head snapped back. "Fuck!" He said as he turned and saw they were quickly approaching the waterfall. "Uh. What do we do?" Demitri asked. Kain clenched his jaw and took a deep breath.

Suddenly, Henry came out of nowhere, racing down past them on horseback. He made it to the edge of the forest and jumped from his horse. He grabbed a broken tree branch from the forest line and held it out to them.

"Grab it as you float by!" Henry shouted while he stretched the branch out into the river.

Kain nodded and steadied his injured left arm. He knew he would have only one chance to get him and Demitri out of this. Once they were passing by the branch, he reached out and barely managed to grab onto a knot at the end of it. Kain pulled against the stick, swinging the two over to the muddy edge of the river as he yelled in pain. Henry helped pull Demitri out of the water while Kain got himself out. Kain crawled out of the river and laid on the grass. He spread his arms out and looked up at the sky as he hyperventilated. Rain was dumping down on him, but he was so exhausted he didn't care.

Once Kain remembered what had happened to Drake, he shot up and screamed, "Commander Henry, where's Drake!? Where'd you leave him?" Henry was on his knees helping Demitri get the water out of his lungs.

The Commander looked over at Kain and answered, "In the first watchtower. Go to him. He needs medical assistance."

Kain nodded to Henry, spun around and ran toward the gates of Fort Malum. Once he reached the entrance, he turned back to see the mayhem behind him. It seemed like an endless number of corpses were now floating through the Tenebris and over the waterfall. The Galgarians were sitting along the river's edge cheering and throwing even more bodies into the water. Kain looked out past them and saw the bodies of royal soldiers spread throughout the grassy battlefield. When he looked at those of his men who had managed to survive and make it back over the river, he saw that most were horrifically wounded, and many were having trouble even walking. Kain turned his head away and passed through the gates.

When Kain reached the first watchtower, a crowd of men were standing in a circle. Kain jogged up to the crowd and pushed the men aside. He looked down and saw Drake on his back breathing softly. The cut on his face had ripped his cheek wide open, and blood was quickly seeping out of him. Kain knelt down next to him and then immediately looked to the other Commanders surrounding him.

"Grab me some bandages. Now!" Kain ordered. A soldier came back almost instantly with a roll of white cloth. "Send word to King Alastor." Kain panted as he patched up Drake's bloody face. "We're going to be needing a lot more men."

PART III

CHAPTER 10

The sound of clashing metal ricocheted throughout the training facility. Kain and his student battled back and forth as a crowd of cadets watched closely. The student continued to press forward, swinging in all directions. Kain blocked the oncoming swings with ease. Finally, their blades stalled against each other.

Kain held their weapons together between them; then he shifted his arms and brought their sword tips to the ground. As he held their blades against the floor, he stretched his foot behind the boys and swiped it, knocking the boy off balance. Kain then pushed against the boy's chest and sent him soaring backwards. The student flopped to the floor while his sword went flying. Kain looked down at the boy, then back over at the group of students huddled together beside the circle line. He reached his hand out to help the young man up.

"If you're locked up like that, never let someone take control of where your swords go. It's you who needs to make that move." Kain instructed. He then sheathed his blade on his back and surveyed the crowd in front of him. "Alright, that'll be all for today. We'll work defensively tomorrow, so make sure to bring your shields."

Kain removed his arm guards and grabbed a rag to wipe the sweat from his face. He shook his wet hair out and slumped down against the wall to rest. The swarm of students in front of him started to trickle out of the training room doors. Kain placed his hand over his eyes and sighed. When he looked up, a man was standing in front of him. The man's hands rested on his hips while his shadow fell over Kain.

"You looked good out there," a shrill voice said.

"What are you doing here Ivan?" Kain snapped. "You don't instruct on Thursdays. And keep your sarcastic fucking comments to yourself. I don't care what you have to say. Ever." Kain threw his sweat rag aside and placed his face back in his hands.

"No, I really mean it this time. Those kids are lucky to have you as their instructor. You certainly show them what not to do." Ivan taunted as he began to pace back and forth in front of Kain. His hands were crossed behind his back, and his long, straight, blonde hair drooped over his face. Beneath his hair Kain could see a smug smile peeking through. "You know Kain, there's something about you that I've just … never liked." Kain clenched his jaw and shook his head.

"Is that so?" Kain shot back. A burst of energy jolted through his body.

Ivan glanced down as his lips curled back into a smirk, he continued, "But the thing is, I don't think you've ever known exactly what it is about you that I don't like." Kain jumped up and met Ivan's gaze. Their eyes locked. Ivan's antagonistic smile stayed planted on his face as Kain's angry stare reflected back at him.

"Oh yeah? And what does it happen to be?" Kain replied while his body tensed. He could feel the white-hot rage begin to fester within him. He held it back with all his might.

"You know, surprisingly, I've thought about you a lot Kain," Ivan said as he looked down at the ground and smiled. He seemed to be holding back laughter. "Since your father was the greatest traitor this Kingdom has ever seen, I've always been curious just how it was that your family was foolish enough to let you make your way to the

Capital in the first place. But then I think I figured it out." Ivan looked up, shook his hair back and matched Kain's glare. Kain's nostrils began to flare while his eyes narrowed. Ivan continued, "Everyone's heard the story of course. The brave, young Kain Villairo desperately tried to protect his poor uncle from the royal soldiers. Although his attempt was ultimately futile, at least now the Kingdom would finally have someone with the true will to fight." Ivan raised his hand and clenched it into a fist. "Marvelous. But there's another part I heard as well. The part nobody seems to talk all that much about. The part where your mother watched, silently, as her only son was given up. Without any fight at all." Ivan was staring at Kain with a sadistic look in his eye. "So I guess I figured it out then. She must have not wanted to save you. That must have been it. That sure was an easy way to get out of dealing with you!" Ivan gripped his stomach and laughed hysterically. He then inched his nose closer to Kain's. Then his face lost all expression; he tilted his head and gnashed his teeth. "What do you think that says about how much she cared for her one and only son?" Kain drew his blade from his back and growled as Ivan stepped away, drawing his. "There he is," Ivan mumbled under his breath as him and Kain began to circle each other.

Kain seethed with anger as he slowly beginning to twirl his sword. "There will come a day where I'll finally be done with you."

"Maybe then you'll actually give me a fight." Ivan shouted back as he lunged at Kain. Their blades instantly clashed. Ivan could feel the power in Kain's swing. He backed off slowly. Kain and Ivan repositioned themselves before engaging once more. Their swords began to expertly dance back and forth with each other. The fighters swung viciously across their bodies as their blades continued to meet. Soon their swords finally stalled against each other. Ivan pulled his sword away from their bind and grazed Kain's arm.

Kain looked down to see blood seeping out from his left bicep. He clenched his jaw and glared at Ivan before launching into an all-out assault. Ivan had to exert all his effort into resisting Kain's blows.

Kain slashed from all directions while Ivan dropped back and met the oncoming swings. Not long after Ivan took the defensive, he began to lose his balance and Kain took notice. Kain slashed high and then circled his swing back down low, slicing Ivan's quad. Ivan's knees buckled as he lost his footing. His hand fell to his waist. Kain turned the angle of his blade and slapped the flat of it against Ivan's hand and knocked his sword away from him. Ivan stumbled back and clutched his bloody leg.

Kain slowly lowered his sword and turned his head away from Ivan. Then he pivoted, stepped forward and struck Ivan across the face with the flat of his blade. Ivan was knocked to the ground where he landed on his back.

Kain put his hands on his hips and stared down at Ivan, shaking his head in disgust. After a few moments, he started walking away from the training circle and toward the exit. He sheathed his sword behind him. Ivan perched up on his hands, growled, and then drew a small dagger from his back and threw it.

Kain froze as he felt the blade rip through the straps on his chest plate and lightly pierce his left trap muscle. He swung his arm over his shoulder and ripped out the dagger. A primal anger overtook him. Kain spun around, raised the knife above his head, and marched toward Ivan who was still on the ground. Ivan started frantically shifting and trying to back away. Fear glistened in his eyes.

"General Villairo!" one of the King's aides yelled from the balcony overlooking the facility. Kain halted with the dagger still raised and clenched in his hand ready to strike. He turned his head steadily up to the man. "The King requests your presence … immediately." Kain looked back at Ivan.

"If you ever try something like that again, I'll use my sword the way it's supposed to be used. I promise you, today is the last time I will ever show you any sort of mercy," Kain snapped. He then snarled and stormed off. He left the training arena and made his way over to the palace. Once he passed through the city square, he jogged up the stairs to the King's podium and then pushed open the doors to the throne room.

"The King is waiting out in the courtyard," said another of the King's aides who stood inside looking at Kain and pointing to his right. Kain nodded and walked toward the archway that led outside. As soon as he reached the courtyard, he saw the blood red robes of the King standing beside a cleanly trimmed row of bushes.

King Alastor turned around and greeted his favorite soldier, "Kain, my boy." The King smiled and reached out his arms.

"Your majesty," Kain said as he placed his hands behind his back and bowed.

"Come now, walk with me. I have good news to share." The King said while waving for Kain to come with him. His robes grazed the floor as they strolled farther into the courtyard. Eight royal guardsmen, covered head to toe in golden bronze armor, followed behind. All that exposed the guards were the thin eye slits in their helmets. They walked robotically in tandem behind Kain and the King. "This war that has long plagued our eastern border is finally coming to an end. We have located Jarin and what remains of the Galgarian army." Kain whipped his head over at King Alastor and raised his eyebrows. "Now, Sir Drake is out in Malshire preparing to finish them once and for all, but he has sent for your help. He thinks it should be you two who end this war, given your history with Jarin." Alastor stopped and turned to Kain. His expression went cold. "I made the promise years ago that I would not stop until I had killed every last one of them. And I by all means intend to keep that promise." King Alastor put his hand on Kain's shoulder. "Don't let me down, son."

"Of course not, my Lord. I'll take the first brigade at daybreak," Kain blurted out. He had become jittery as he smiled. He had been away from battle for almost a year and didn't think he would get the chance to go back again.

"No, no, you will take the third brigade with you," the King said sternly as his posture stiffened.

"But, my men—" the King waved his hand and cut Kain off.

Alastor continued, "This war has left us in desperate need of soldiers; we must maintain a strong defense of the city and keep our occupying troops strong. The outer villages must remain well protected." Alastor put his head down as he walked toward the balcony. "I am sending Ivan and Demitri to lead their brigades out to the villages tomorrow to recruit a new batch of boys, but until we have replenished our forces, you will have to lead the third brigade. We must maintain the appearance of a full and capable military force. And you have certainly turned the first brigade into our most excellent display of soldiers." Kain hesitantly nodded as the King looked at him and smiled. "This Kingdom knows all you have done for us in this war, and I assure you, it will not go without recognition."

"Thank you, my Lord," Kain replied while bowing his head to King Alastor.

"I ask just one more thing." Kain raised his eyebrows. King Alastor's face once again turned cold and sharp before he added, "Bring me Jarin's head."

Kain squinted and furrowed his brow. He nodded and answered, "We'll ride at dawn."

After being dismissed by the King, Kain headed back to the military barracks. When he got there, he went inside his room and took off his armor. He hung it on the wooden stand in the corner beside his mirror. Once he unsheathed his sword and placed it back on his mantle, he grabbed his robe and headed out the door.

Kain walked down the hall and knocked on the neighboring door to him. After a few moments, the latch was unlocked, and the wooden door flung open. A man with short, black hair stood in the doorway. The man was about six feet tall, very lean and a tan robe was cloaked over him.

"So, the King's sending you to the outer villages tomorrow?" Kain asked. Demitri nodded slowly.

"Looks like it. There hasn't been a draft in over a decade. Not since we were snatched up," Demitri said with a grin. He then hit Kain on the shoulder and added, "We must really need the numbers." Kain tilted his head to the side and scrunched his face.

"I guess. I'm not sure who's really a threat to us once we finish the Galgarians off once and for all. But it sounds like King Alastor doesn't want to take any chances," Kain said as he put his hands on his hips.

"Is he sending you to recruit as well?" Demitri asked. "He didn't mention it."

Kain replied, "No, Sir Drake requested I be there when we take out Jarin and the rest of those stragglers. I couldn't believe it when he told me. I haven't been out there in almost a year. I'm sick of instructing. It's going to be so much fun to be back in the action, especially in a situation like this. Get to kill as many Galgarians as I can get my hands on."

"Honestly. I only got two years of being a Commander out of this war. Sounds like we need another one." Demitri joked.

"Well, I figured we'd go to the bar. Have a little celebration now that this all is truly coming to an end. Why don't we go to the usual spot?" Kain then waved his arm, inviting Demitri outside.

"It would be my absolute honor to have a drink with a general," Demitiri said mockingly. Kain punched his arm.

"Fuck you. Come on, let's go."

Demitri agreed, stepped outside and shut his door behind him. The two of them headed down the hallway.

CHAPTER 11

E arly the next morning, Kain made his way down to the city square where he found the third brigade waiting for him. Next to his army, two smaller groups of soldiers were also standing by at the ready. Empty carriages littered the square. As Kain inspected the other groups of soldiers, Demitri came walking toward him.

"Got a killer fucking headache thanks to you," Demitri said as he rubbed his forehead.

Kain smiled and shook hands with Demitri while admiring the staff hanging on his back. The weapon was a long, wooden rod with short blades that tipped each end. One side of each blade was sharp, whereas the other side had a metal ball welded into it making each end of the rod useful as a club.

Demitri stared out at the sea of men before him. He placed both hands on the top of his shaved head while he admired the legion. He glanced back at Kain and squinted before saying, "Well, I sure wish I was heading out to battle. And not to the God damned outer villages." Demitri smiled. "No offense, I mean."

Kain laughed, raised his eyebrows, and then responded, "Hey, not all of us can be from the luxurious south. And don't worry; it'll be fine. Try and get us a good batch out there at least."

"Hopefully," Demitri mumbled as he kicked the cobblestone surface beneath him. "I'll tell you though, I highly doubt we'll end up getting another Kain Villairo out of it." Kain smiled and shook his head.

"And what is it you will be doing Villairo?" Ivan asked while snaking his way through the city square and over to Kain and Demitri.

"Off to help the King's Hand end this war," Kain proclaimed. He strapped his chest plate tight before looking up intensely at his rival. Ivan growled and gnashed his teeth.

"That should be me out there, and you know it." Ivan snarled and pressed his finger into the lion crest on Kain's torso before turning away. While Ivan walked toward his army, he called back to Demitri and waved his finger in the air. "You take your men to the western villages; my men and I will head north."

Demitri squinted and shook his head while watching Ivan strut away. "At least I don't have to fucking travel with him," he said under his breath.

Kain nodded and replied, "Damn right. Safe travels Demitri. Good luck out there." The two shook hands one last time.

"Go win this war for us all," Demitri said before heading off to tend to his faction of men. The three armies soon marched out of the castle until eventually breaking off into their separate directions.

It took Kain and his men all day to reach Malshire. By the evening sunset they had finally reached the campgrounds just outside the village. The soldiers stationed there were scattered throughout a large grassy field where they seemed to be just beginning to settle down, getting ready to rest. At the edge of the meadow was a cluster of fancy tents that sat along the perimeter of where the soldiers were now lying down to sleep.

Once Kain arrived, he tied up his horse and headed into the Commander's tent. When he walked through the fabric entrance, the crowd of men stopped talking and immediately turned to him. The King's Hand stood from his seat and rushed over to Kain with a massive grin on his face. The scar Jarin had etched into Drake's cheek all those years ago starkly protruded as he smiled.

"General Villairo! Good to have you back," Drake said with outstretched arms. His golden gauntlet covered his left hand. "I was adamant it had to be me and you who ended this war. Luckily King Alastor agreed!"

Kain answered, "Sir Drake, it is now and always has been an honor to fight by your side. I can't imagine not being here for it either." He smiled and bowed his head slightly; then he gave his old mentor a hug. Drake was still much bigger than Kain, and he completely enveloped his protege during their hug. Kain scanned the others in the room while the two broke from their embrace.

Drake then turned to the table of Commanders, put his arm around Kain and announced, "I found this one when he was only a boy! All the way out in the prairies, Valgard, wasn't it? What a soldier he's become. General Villairo, you have indeed become a merciless man." Drake looked down at Kain then back at the Commanders. "I can't tell you how many times he's saved my ass. I wouldn't even want to admit it!" Drake shook his head and grinned. "I've trained him since he was just an Elevener! The best swordsman on the peninsula!" Kain smiled and looked at the ground. Some of the Commanders in the room silently glared at him. Other Commanders that Kain had previously served alongside nodded pleasantly at him. Many of the skeptical ones had hints of jealousy in their faces. Most of them were still much older than Kain.

"So then, what's our battle plan?" Kain asked while he walked over to the table and inspected the map. Figurines were spread out across the table that laid out their various positions.

"Well, our spies have tracked the last remaining Galgarians here,"

Drake said as he pointed to the town of Grastian; it was quite far east from the border where the Nymean Peninsula connected to the mainland. "Once we get there, we'll swarm the city and smoke them out. There shouldn't be more than a couple hundred of them left." Drake looked up at the Commanders surrounding the table. "This will all be over soon. I promise you, Jarin will pay the price for the men of Nymea that he's killed."

Kain's focus remained intensely fixated on the war map. He evaluated their positions on the board, reading all the notes that had been sketched out during prior discussions. He looked around at the men sitting at the table.

"And how far is the journey to Grastian from here?" Kain asked.

One of the Commanders spoke up, "About a day's travel if we really hurry. We were planning to leave at dawn. We should get there by sunset tomorrow evening."

Kain nodded and replied, "And we're sure Jarin is there?" He looked back at Drake.

"Certain. And he's not getting away, ever again," Drake promised. He then laughed and folded his arms. Kain gave a half smile as he continued inspecting the battle map.

"Well, then me and the third brigade will be ready at dawn," Kain said as he looked up and began walking away from the table. Just before he reached the exit, he whipped his head back and asked, "Oh right, is my tent prepared?"

"The one to the left of mine; yours has black trimming on the cloth." Drake said.

Kain nodded to Drake and brushed the curtain aside as he left the tent. Kain walked through the grass and into his own tent. His bed had been laid out for him, and an armor rack stood in the corner. He placed his gear on the wooden rack, blew out the candle and got in bed.

Kain awoke to the sound of soldiers readying their gear outside of his tent. Dawn was just beginning to break. He jumped out of bed and started to drape his chest plate over himself. He slipped on his arm and shin guards, tied his boots, then sheathed his sword behind his back before pushing through the cloth door of his tent. His armor was still in the same style it had always been. Lightweight and jet black.

As Kain got outside, he looked over to the east and saw the group of Commanders mounting their horses beside their own cluster of tents. He then hopped onto the back of his stallion and rode over to be beside the King's Hand. Once they had gathered the army into form, they began their journey to Grastian.

CHAPTER 12

After passing through all of the towns west of the Capital city and gathering the boys from each of them, Demitri and his men eventually found themselves stumbling upon Kain's hometown of Valgard as the evening sun was beginning to set. The royal soldiers and the citizens were now both gathering in the town square.

Once he had entered the town square, Demitri jumped down from his horse and called out to the people of the village, "Your King, Alastor, has called upon your young men for compulsory military service. All boys aged eleven to twenty-two will be required to serve a seven-year term in the Royal Army. The war effort against the Galgarians is finally coming to an end. Now, it's time we begin the process of rebuilding Nymea's forces." The young boys throughout the town square looked to their mothers and fathers in fear while gasps and whispers seeped out from the crowd. Demitri seemed unphased by the response as he continued to address the people. "We have been traveling for many hours to reach the prairies, and we wish for a night of rest before we load up our new recruits. You will all quarter as many soldiers as your homes will allow, and in the morning, your boys will come with us to join the ranks of the Royal Army." Demitri turned away from the villagers while soldiers began barging into the homes that surrounded the town square.

A young woman stood at the back of the crowd of townspeople. Her face was frozen in a state of horror while she backed away slowly. She then rushed over to the town stable, jumped on a horse and headed out into the farmlands. Soon, she came upon a small shack where she dismounted from her horse and burst through the front door of the hut.

"Bruce, they're here!"

"Alice! Who's here? What's going on?" Bruce gasped as he shot up from his seat and put his hands on the table.

"The Royal Army; they're here; they're going to take our boys again. Just like they took Kain. My little brother, he's only thirteen … Bruce, we can't let them take him!" Alice was nearly in tears while she clasped her hands together and begged for Bruce's help.

Bruce looked at the ground as he chewed on his fingers, "No," he said. He then moved his eyes to meet Alice's gaze. He shook his head. "No Alice, they're not taking anybody. Not again." Bruce put his hand to the side of his cheek and rubbed his blond beard. "I need you to tell me exactly what their Commander said." When Alice relayed the orders that Demitri had given, Bruce smiled.

"Why are you smiling? What does it mean?" Alice asked, still in a panic. She then ran her hands through her hair as her body continued to tremble.

Bruce stared at her and responded, "If the soldiers are being quartered, that means they'll be expecting the men in the village to be sleeping outside tonight. With them separated from the army, we can easily gather the men who are willing to fight without even waking the royal soldiers. I need you to go back to the village. Tell Ambrose, James, Leo, and John to meet me here as soon as possible." A look of worry remained stuck on Alice's face. Bruce reassured her, "Don't worry. I'm not going to let them take him." Alice gave a half-hearted smile and rushed out the door. She leapt up on her horse and rode back to Valgard.

Once she returned to the village, Alice immediately notified Bruce's friends. As soon as they were told, they sped out to Bruce's farm. When they arrived, Bruce, Ben and Meredith were all sitting at the table. They glanced up as the four men stormed in.

"Sit down." Bruce ordered calmly. The friends anxiously gathered around and sat. Bruce gave them a stern look and patted his hand on the table. "The Royal Army will not be taking our boys."

"But what can we do? How do we stop them?" Ambrose said while perched in his seat.

"The men will be sleeping outside, yes?" Bruce asked. His friends nodded.

"Perfect," Ben interjected. "This really will be easier than I thought." He glanced over at his nephew.

Bruce paused and looked around at the four men before continuing, "First, there's something you all need to know. Ben here was one of the men who led the rebellion back in the day." The men around the table gasped as they stared at Ben.

"You fought with Victor Villairo in the Great Rebellion?" James asked as his mouth fell open.

Ben looked up and smiled. "I did."

Bruce's eyes fluttered around the room before he added, "There's one more thing I feel you all should know before we go any further … Victor Villairo … is my father as well."

"What? Your father? But … I thought Kain was your cousin? Ben isn't your father?" James asked, looking flustered. The four men were stunned by the revelation.

"It's true," Meredith spoke up. "Once the town found out about Kain, we had to try and convince everyone that Bruce was Ben's son. To still at least try and keep Victor's paternity a secret for Bruce. But in truth, Kain and Bruce are twins." The four men stared at Bruce.

Ben cut in, "Anyway, we need to focus." He placed his hands

on the table and continued, "We have to quickly inform the men in the town about this operation without the soldiers overhearing." He turned to Bruce's friends. "That will be your guys' job. Me and Bruce will collect as many weapons as we can and store them out by the pond. That's where we'll meet tonight. We'll need to gather the men in increments so as not to wake the soldiers. How many soldiers are there anyway?" The four men looked back and forth at each other.

"Maybe fifty?" James said.

Ben smiled and nodded. "Good," he said as he stood up and began pacing around the room. He folded his hands together and kept his gaze fixed down on the ground. "Now, if we are going to do this, you all must know there is no turning back. This will be a declaration of war on the Kingdom. Your punishment will be death if not far worse. Do you understand?" The men nodded. "Alright then. There will undoubtedly be watchmen patrolling the town tonight. You four will need to take them out before we can bring the townsmen back to the pond. After the watchmen have been dealt with, alert the villagers that have joined the cause. We'll have as much armor and weaponry as we can find waiting for them. Each of you take a faction of men out to the pond, one at a time. Stagger the timing, but be efficient. We'll need everyone to be ready to strike just before dawn."

Ambrose, James, Leo, and John headed back to the village to spread the word and wait for nightfall. A few hours after sunset, the royal soldiers eventually began to make their way inside and retire to bed. Four men soon emerged to take their shifts as watchmen. They slowly began to walk through the streets of Valgard as the men of the village laid outside their homes, sleeping on the dirt. The town quickly fell eerily silent. The only sound that could be heard was the crunching of gravel beneath the soldiers' feet as they lurked through the streets.

After a few hours, the second group of watchmen came in to take over the shift. Once they exchanged positions with the previous guards, the new soldiers started to patrol the town. The four rebels lingered in the shadows, waiting for their moment. They inspected the watchmen closely, examining how they walked sleepily through the streets and alleyways of the village. Soon enough, the shift in the soldiers' posture and focus indicated that they had finally lost all sense of urgency.

Ambrose was the first to attack; he crept out of the darkness where he was hiding and began stalking the soldier who had begun walking in front of him. Ambrose had removed his shoes so as not to create extra noise. He had a dagger in his hand, ready to strike. He crouched and paced behind the soldier silently. When he was close enough, he reached around the man and sliced the knife along his throat. Ambrose covered the guard's mouth with his open hand to stifle any screams. The soldier buckled and reached for his neck as it gushed blood. He fell back into Ambrose's arms where he was then set on the ground gently and dragged into an alley.

James was waiting behind the corner of a shop that bordered the main strip of the town, clutching his sword in his hands. He positioned it upright and readied himself for a swing. The crunch beneath the shoulder's bootstraps echoed in the night. It was getting louder, and once he knew the soldier was imminently close by, he turned the corner and swiped cleanly through the soldier's neck. There was no time for a scream as the man's head separated from his body and dropped to the floor. James carried his corpse into the darkness.

Leo had set a trap in one of the dark alleys off the main road. He had dug a hole and set up a trip wire which activated a sharpened rake to swing through its target. On the other side of the alley, he was hiding behind a hay bale waiting to send the final cut into the soldier once the trap had been set.

When Leo heard the nearby soldier approach, Leo kicked up some rocks, triggering him to come inspect. Soon enough, the soldier rushed around the corner, fell into the shallow hole and activated the trap. Forks stabbed through his lower abdomen as Leo appeared instantly from his hiding spot to slice off his head and avoid a scream.

It was now up to John to take out the last of the guards. He had been watching his guard patiently. He saw that the soldier would often take short breaks. The man would sit on the porch of the tavern and sip from a wooden bowl. When the soldier got up from his break and began patrolling the streets once more, John crept over to the bowl and dumped grindings of water hemlock into it. After mixing it around, he slipped back into the darkness to wait.

The soldier returned to his resting spot within the hour and sipped his drink as if nothing was unusual. Fifteen minutes following the ingestion, he began to shake violently. The veins in his neck bulged as he gripped his stomach. He started foaming at the mouth before crouching over and falling to the ground. After a series of convulsive shakes, his body stiffened, and John dragged his corpse under the porch.

Once the four men successfully cleared out the watchmen, they took turns rallying the villagers and bringing them out to meet Bruce and Ben. When the townsmen had finally congregated at the pond, Bruce addressed the newly formed militia, "If we're going to overpower the royal soldiers, we have to be effective. As soon as dawn breaks, you need to be ready at each of your homes. Since you'll all know the layout of your own houses best, storm in and take out the soldiers as they sleep. Be quick. We must kill at least half of them immediately if we're going to stand a chance. Don't let your armor clank, and make sure to walk softly. You'll all wait for my signal once everyone is in position. Now, gear up and prepare."

The men began putting on the ragged armor that Ben and Bruce had been able to scavenge. Each leaned over and picked up one of the weapons that now littered the ground. Once they were all properly fitted, they started their creep into town.

After sneaking their way back into the village, each man lined up outside his home. They all turned to see Bruce in the middle of the town square, counting down from three with his hand. As soon as his hand turned to a fist, the men charged inside. Screams and metal clanking erupted from inside the homes as the villagers stabbed into the sleeping soldiers.

After only a few moments, some of the townsmen had been bested by the delirious soldiers. Those surviving soldiers then poured out into the streets trying to get a grasp on the situation. Bruce and the other villagers that didn't invade awaited their approach. Bruce clashed with the first few soldiers to come his way. They were disoriented from their abrupt wake up and Bruce sliced cleanly through the first three to attack him. The other townsmen spread out to meet the oncoming soldiers.

The King's army had indeed been cut in half by their ambush, and the few that remained were now being held up by Bruce and the other villagers in the town square. Soon, Demitri came racing out from one of the houses to join the battle. He easily cut down any villager that was foolish enough to stand in his path. Bruce turned to see his men in serious trouble and ran over to confront Demitri.

Once he had defeated the first wave of townsmen coming his way, Demitri turned his attention to Bruce. Demitri rushed him and began twirling his dual-edged staff. Bruce lifted his sword to block the first swing. Demitri spun his staff back and forth while Bruce used his sword and shield to halt the blades coming at each side of him. Bruce had never seen a weapon like this before, and he was having trouble freeing himself up to take the offensive. He continued to step back and block the endless swings coming at him from all directions now.

Finally, Demitri backed off and repositioned to get a wider grip on his spear. Now the attacks came at an even faster rate, but Demitiri was exposed. As he lowered the staff horizontally, Bruce slashed down ferociously, splitting the weapon in two. Demitri looked down in shock as Bruce suddenly rushed toward him. Demitri was using his now split weapon to block, but he couldn't keep it up for long. Bruce pressed on and after sending Demitri off balance, he spun and cut down on Demitri's left arm. Demitri's hand dropped to the ground as he screamed in pain. Blood poured from his arm. He could no longer resist Bruce's blows. Soon Demitri was knocked to his knees and Bruce plunged his sword through Demitri's chest. Bruce pulled out the blade and Demitri fell face first into the dirt.

Breathing heavily, Bruce bent over and put his hands on his hips. After a few moments he relaxed and straightened his posture. He sheathed his sword and turned around to see many villagers standing victorious over the bodies of royal soldiers scattered throughout the town. The villagers looked at him while they panted and wiped the sweat from their faces. Ambrose, James, Leo and John rushed up to Bruce, as did all the remaining villagers who survived. The women and children who had been sleeping inside during the ambush cautiously crept out from their houses to see what was going on.

Bruce stood and surveyed the remaining men; blood and sweat dripped from his blond beard. He took off his creamy white chest plate and threw it aside along with his arm guards. The sun was just beginning to rise, and the golden shine lit up the clouds behind Valgard. Bruce looked around, scratched his short hair and then addressed the crowd of men standing before him.

"It looks like we managed to only lose a few," Bruce said. He was still panting and trying to catch his breath as he knelt down next to a fallen young villager and checked for a pulse. "That's a relief; we're going to need every soldier we can find." He stood and turned to face the rest of the village which had now formed a massive crowd in front of him. "You're all brave soldiers, and I am proud to have fought with each and every one of you. Go now; be with your families, with your boys. Get some rest; I'll be back soon to discuss our next move. But remember, this has only just begun. Prepare yourselves; we're going to have some nasty fights ahead of us."

Bruce walked over to the carriages filled with young boys that had been taken from the other western villages and cut the restraints on the carriage. The boys trickled out slowly while looking around at Bruce and the militiamen. They then formed a huddle.

Bruce waved his hand and yelled, "You are all free to go back to your homes. Or, you may stay with us and fight. If you return home, I can assure you, you will not be spared from this battle. For if you return home, you will likely be rounded up once more and again be made to fight in the Royal Army. Alastor may even consider you traitors if you do not make your way back to the Capital at this very moment. Either way, the choice is yours." The boys continued to stand there silently. Soon, a few began to step forward. Then nearly all joined in.

One of the older boys at the front of the pack was staring at Bruce. "We want to fight. Not for King Alastor, but for you," the boy said as he gave a confident nod. Bruce nodded back.

Bruce looked around at the boys and responded, "Excellent. Those of you over fifteen will fight alongside us in combat. All of you younger ones—we'll need your help with resource production and communications." The crowd of boys smiled.

Bruce and his four friends then headed back to Ben's house. After explaining what had just happened, Bruce asked what they needed to do next. Ben stood there with a slight smile on his face while his hand held his chin.

After a few moments of silence, Ben spoke, "We need to act quickly. If this rebellion is contained to just this town, we'll all be burnt at the stake, everyone in the village, just to be made an example of. We need to take this fight out to the other villages. There has to be more revolts against the other occupying soldiers. We can't let ourselves become an isolated target. Does anyone have connections to nearby towns?"

"I have cousins in Polissa; they'd surely be willing to fight," Ambrose offered.

"My parents and brother live in Shoria. I know he has other friends that would join us," James added.

Ben clenched his hand into a fist and shouted, "Great! Go to them, spread word of the rebellion. Tell them what the Kingdom is going to take from them; remind them of what has already been taken, and get them to help us fight back."

Bruce looked at his uncle and scrunched his face, "Uncle, they must've rounded up half the boys in the outer villages by now. How are we ever going to get enough soldiers to march on the Capital?"

Ben shook his head and quickly replied, "We're not going to take the Capital that way. Don't you see? That was our mistake all those years ago." He patted Bruce on the arm. "We were never going to win by taking them head-on. And even if we had been able to win, what is one dictatorship for another?"

Bruce cut in, "Hold on. Wasn't the whole point of the rebellion to take down the monarchy?"

Ben waved his hand dismissively before answering, "Yes, but think about it from the perspective of those who actually live in the Capital. They would never have seen it as a victory. Undoubtedly a new system of government would have been put in place and who is to say they would have agreed with it? No, no, the secret here, is to turn the people of the Kingdom, and the Capital in particular, against the King and the Kingdom itself. We must destabilize them from the inside."

"Well how are we going to do that?" Leo yelled. "The people there are so twisted by their propaganda that they think King Alastor is a hero!"

Ben paused for a moment. He then slowly raised his pointer finger out from his fist and said, "There's a small village just outside the Capital. Its crop yield is what provides around ninety percent of the Capital city's food supply. Primarily the food supply of the peasants inside the actual castle walls. We'll capture this city from its occupation and burn their crop fields."

Bruce interjected instantly, "You want to starve the people?"

Ben looked back at his nephew calmly and answered, "It won't take long for people to turn against the King this way." He turned to other men and said, "And as you already pointed out Leo, the people of the Capital are blindly convinced of their King's benevolence. Well, that may be true, but it'll be difficult for him to continue to convince the people of his greatness while their children have nothing to eat." It seemed the men were beginning to understand the tactic. Ben continued, "This foolishly drawn-out war with the Galgarians has cost the army of this Kingdom greatly. If they're implementing a military draft, they must be truly desperate to rebuild. This is our chance. We need to strike quickly. Gather up as many men as possible who are willing to fight in Polissa and Shoria and take out their occupying troops." Everyone around the table continued listening intently. "We need to be careful; our army must never congregate. That was another mistake we made. Between attacks and battles, you all must disappear, everyone. Blend in with the villagers; if they can't find us, they can't fight us. We need to be invisible." Ben turned to Bruce. "Start operating communications out of Polissa as soon as you can. Only allow talks of strategy to occur between us. Come and report back to me once you've gone and freed the villages. Now, go!" Ben banged his hand on the table as the men dispersed.

Bruce stayed behind. He folded his arms and slowly turned his head to his uncle.

"Do you really think we can do this, Ben?" Bruce asked.

Ben put his hand to his chin and stared at his nephew. "If there's a time to try, it's now."

CHAPTER 13

Down on the western edge of Galgaria, Kain and Drake were finally approaching the outskirts of Grastian. The town sat tucked between the mountains in a small and grassy valley. An open strip ran directly through the center of the village, with small huts and shacks making up the bulk of each row of the town. A small stone church stood at the very back of the strip.

The mountain shadows had now engulfed the village as the sun was nearly about to set. The sky quickly began to shift into a bright orange collage against the backs of the royal soldiers. The men continued to cautiously march straight through the village strip.

"Looks awfully barren," Kain said while surveying the shops and houses beside him. The Commanders trotted eerily through the main strip of the town while the legion of soldiers followed behind. A few villagers stared out of their windows watching the army pass through the town.

"Oh they're here. I can feel it." Drake replied while he rode side by side with Kain. The soft clicking of hooves echoed throughout the valley. As they marched through the town, more townspeople soon peeked their heads out of their doorways, curious as to what Nymea's army could be doing in their small village. The town remained suspiciously silent.

"Soldiers! Check the houses!" Drake's voice boomed through the town. The men began inspecting the homes while a small number of villagers filtered out into the streets. After a few minutes of searching, one of the Commanders stuck his head out from one of the doorways and called for Drake.

"Sir Drake, it seems they're not here," the Commander shouted.

Kain and Drake quickly glanced over at each other, both sensing something was wrong. Suddenly, the now dimly lit sky began to illuminate. Their heads snapped upwards to see flaming arrows soaring through the air. The arrows quickly began to fall onto the roofs of the buildings. The town erupted in flames as the arrows lit fire to oil which had been poured all over the town. A ring of fire soon encircled the village as droves of enemy soldiers began storming the village from the hills behind them. Bone chilling shrieks came from the men and villagers who had been caught inside the now burning buildings.

The remaining royal soldiers spun around and headed straight for the fire wall to meet the oncoming army. Kain yelled for the nearest group of cavalry men on horseback to follow him, exit from the other side of the town, and flank the enemy soldiers.

Drake raced toward the fire wall with a few hundred men following. The royal soldiers had barely crossed the fire line when the two armies crashed into each other. Frontline soldiers instantly met their demise as the two armies collided.

Kain was rounding the corner on horseback with around twenty men. Their squadron began charging toward the wall of enemy soldiers. The Galgarians shifted their form to brace for Kain's oncoming faction. Kain drew his sword and began cutting into the men below.

Kain kept fighting from atop his horse until a spear was finally sent through the lungs of his stallion. The horse buckled and tumbled to the ground. Kain jumped off the horse, rolled, and regained his footing.

When he looked up, he found himself face to face with the general of the Galgarian army, Jarin. They began cautiously circling each other.

Jarin took his helmet off to reveal his cold and brutish face. He threw the helmet to the ground. His red hair was braided down his back and his beard was already drenched in blood. He wore no chest plate, just a green vest along with his massive arm pads. He had his short, pointed sword down at his side. He spat on the ground and growled. Kain looked back at him with an equally grimacing stare. Jarin pounded his chest and then readied his sword. He held his hands up by his ear; his blade was now pointed directly at Kain's head.

Before the two men could engage, Drake looked over and saw their standoff. He immediately yelled out, "Kain! He's mine!"

Drake sprinted over and instantly inserted himself into the fight. Drake and Jarin began trading blows as Kain started to relax his stance. Drake seemed to have the advantage initially. Jarin was clearly fighting defensively, using his arm pads to block most of the swings. Drake pressed forward and continued sending strikes at Jarin, coming at him from all directions.

Jarin began to counter and slow the tempo. He started swinging and stabbing as hard as he possibly could, but Drake easily managed to hold his ground. After a few missed swings by Jarin, Drake began to pound his sword down on Jarin with incredible force. Drake swung so hard that upon impact with Jarin's armguard, the swing knocked Jarin back and sent his body rotating. Drake raised his blade over his head. Jarin was still crouched with his back turned. As Drake swung down to deliver the final blow, Jarin spun around and sliced Drake's stomach just below his chest plate.

"No!" Kain screamed. He rushed in as Drake collapsed in a pool of blood. Kain gripped his sword with both hands and swung relentlessly at Jarin. Kain unleashed his anger and put Jarin back on his heels. Jarin finally started to show signs of tiring, but Kain was just getting started. That same white-hot rage burnt through his entire body as he sent slashes coming from both high and low. Kain then locked their swords, disengaged, spun and leapt off his left foot. He bashed down on Jarin's arm, denting the metal.

When Jarin was able to finally get a horizontal swing off, he took aim for Kain's left side. Kain blocked the blow and while Jarin was still completely extended and exposed, he spun off their stalled blades and sliced down on Jarin's arm. It fell onto the ground as blood poured out of him. Jarin screamed and gripped his shoulder. Kain charged at him. Jarin turned to run. Kain pulled his dagger from its sheath and threw it, pinning Jarin in the back. Jarin's body tensed and he tripped over himself, falling face first into the dirt. Kain gripped his sword with both hands and started hacking into Jarin. Blood spattered in all directions as swings kept coming down on the now deceased Galgarian general.

After what seemed like minutes of bashing into Jarin's lifeless body, Kain finally came to a stop. He rose and turned his head slowly. His terrifying scowl was stained red. He pulled his dagger from Jarin's corpse and scanned the battlefield. He was brought out of his trance once he noticed the clashing of men all around him. He dove back into the fight and started slicing at the crowd while the rest of his men swarmed the leftover Galgarians.

An enemy soldier rushed up to Kain, swinging a spear at his head. Kain raised his sword to block the swipe. He knocked the spear away, grabbed the soldier's arm and rolled him over his back. As the man fell to the ground, Kain plunged his sword down into his chest.

Kain looked up and saw two soldiers coming at him from opposite sides. Kain drew his dagger and ran toward the soldier coming to his left. He tossed his dagger over his shoulder to his right, sticking the other soldier in the forehead. With his right hand he slashed at the soldier he was charging toward. The man backed away; his throat barely missed the tip of Kain's sword, but Kain redirected his blade downward and stabbed the man in the foot.

The Galgarian screamed in pain as he dropped to his knee. Kain pulled the sword out and got behind the man. Kain put his arm over the soldier's neck and held him tight. He looked over and saw Drake lying in the grass across the field. Rage consumed him as he brought the blade of his sword up to the man's throat and slowly cut it open. Kain took solace in the man's agony as the blood soon started to pour from his neck. Kain kicked the dead body to the ground.

Kain walked over to the other soldier and pulled his dagger out of the man's bloody skull. Another group of Galgarians were charging at him. Kain threw his dagger once more, nailing the target in the heart. He sprinted toward the other two.

The first Galgarian swung at Kain's head, but Kain ducked the swing, grabbed the back of the man's neck and slammed it down onto his knee. The man bounced back and onto the ground. The last soldier in the pack sliced at Kain, grazing his chest plate.

Kain backed away and the two were now staring each other down. The soldier leapt at Kain and swung his sword down on him. Kain raised his blade to meet the blow. He disarmed the man and gripped him by the throat before sticking his sword through the man's chest.

Kain dropped the corpse, looked around and saw that most of the combat was finally beginning to wind down. The royal soldiers were finishing off what few Galgarians were left. Bodies had piled up throughout the field.

By the end of the fight, Kain and only about fifty men were still standing. They looked out to see the town incinerated along with nearly all his soldiers who had been stuck inside. A few burnt corpses of villagers were scattered throughout the streets as well. The flames had nearly died out at that point, but the town had been torched by the fire. Most of the loosely built wooden huts had collapsed in on themselves. Only a few stone structures remained intact. Villagers and their children stood outside of their destroyed homes. The families clutched each other in fear.

After briefly looking at the destruction of the town, Kain ran over to Drake. He knelt next to his friend and held Drake's head up. Drake was still alive, but just barely. His stomach was completely exposed, and the blood he had been coughing up surrounded his mouth. He looked into Kain's eyes, removed the gauntlet on his hand and handed it to Kain.

"Take it." Drake pleaded.

Kain reached out and grabbed the golden gauntlet. Drake choked out one last breath before closing his eyes for the final time. The remaining soldiers slowly circled their former Chief General. Kain stayed there on his knees, angry and fighting back tears. His body trembled as he gripped the grass.

Kain let out a sigh of exhaustion, re-centered himself and yelled back to his men with his eyes still shut. "Set up camp for the night. We'll start our journey home to the Capital tomorrow."

What remained of the Royal Army began collecting the armor from the dead and then set up their tents. Kain walked over to the carriage cart and pulled out a shovel. He came back next to Drake and started to dig.

A young soldier crept up behind Kain and asked, "General, shouldn't we bring him back to the Capital for a royal burial?"

Kain stopped and looked at the kid before responding, "Drake would want to be laid to rest here. Out on the battlefield." The soldier nodded and walked away.

After Kain finished digging his old friend's grave, he called to a few soldiers to help him move Drake's body. They set him gently on the ground. Kain stared at Drake's still body and began to shake. He closed his eyes as two small streams of tears ran down his face. Kain pulled out his dagger and put it in Drake's hands.

CHAPTER 14

T wo days later, at the Capital, a messenger had made his way into the throne room to inform the King of the recent events in the outer villages. Advisors surrounded Alastor as he sat upon his throne with his legs crossed, staring at the dirt beneath his fingernails. Upon the arrival of the messenger, King Alastor raised his hand to silence his cabinet. He motioned for the messenger to come forward.

"What is it?" Alastor asked.

"My Lord, there seems to be … stirrings in the outer villages." The messenger explained. The King tilted his head and scowled.

"Stirrings? What is that supposed to mean?" Alastor snapped. He was perched on his throne, grabbing the armrests.

The messenger lowered his head and continued, "It appears, some sort of a rebellion has begun." The King stood from his seat, now shaking in fury.

"Where? Get our remaining men in order, and send them out to the village at once." Alastor commanded. The messenger now looked even more concerned. He shivered as he stared at the ground. A single drop of sweat trickled down his face.

"My Lord, this … seems to not be isolated to one village. The occupying troops in all of Polissa, Valgard and Shoria have been slain, including … Demitri and his entire faction of the army you sent."

"What!?" the King shouted. The messenger winced.

"We don't know how many more villages are in contact with these rebels, but we do believe more attacks are imminent, sir." The messenger continued to tremble before King Alastor. The King stood in silence as he stared at the red carpet below him.

Alastor sat back against his throne and scratched the short, gray hairs on his chin and said, "Send a pigeon for Ivan. Recall his army to the Capital. We can't afford to lose any more men. And if this has indeed spread, we need our army concentrated, at least for now. General Villairo and Sir Drake should be arriving momentarily. We'll brief them when they have all returned." King Alastor waved his hand and the messenger rushed out of the throne room.

Within the next hour, Kain and his army had reached the Capital. The King was waiting with his royal guards in the center of the city square as they rode in. He initially appeared pleased by his general's victorious return, but as soon as he noticed the tiny portion of his army that remained, and the gauntlet in Kain's hand, his mood shifted. Alastor's mouth fell open and his eyes slowly widened.

"What … what happened?" the King hissed. Kain got down from his horse and handed Drake's gauntlet to the King. Kain stared at the ground.

"It was a suicide mission. They lit the town ablaze as soon as we arrived. We had our backs against the wall the entire time. They must've known we were coming. It was Jarin who killed Drake." Kain explained. He then took a deep breath and shut his eyes. "We took no prisoners."

The King squinted and gnashed his teeth before responding, "Ivan and his men will be returning later this evening. When he arrives, both of you head straight to the throne room." The King turned and stormed out of the city square. He began marching up the balcony and back to his palace as his royal guards followed behind. Kain sighed and rolled his eyes. He headed back through the city to his barrack.

After a few hours of relaxing and tending to his injuries, Kain heard a knock at his door. A royal advisor came in to tell him Ivan and his men had returned to the Capital and that he and the King were awaiting Kain's arrival in the throne room. Kain threw on his robe and went to meet them.

When Kain got to the doors of the throne room, he stood outside for a moment. He took a deep breath, pushed the doors aside and rushed up the red carpet. Ivan was standing at the base of the stairs. Kain went to stand next to him and then removed his hood. Neither said a word to each other while they waited. The King looked back and forth at them.

"We are faced with a series of … unique challenges, at the moment," Alastor said as he tapped his fingers together. Kain and Ivan stayed silent. "Our army has taken greater losses than we originally anticipated. Although we made some progress in our recruitment from the northern villages, the boys we gained are a long way from being battle ready. We had been preparing to rebuild at the conclusion of this war. But that was all with the assumption of a period of peacetime. And it doesn't look like we will be having that peace after all. It appears, a rebellion has begun in the outer villages. Demitri and all his men were slaughtered yesterday at one of the western villages, and the boys they took have likely already been freed." Kain gasped. His eyes widened as he took in the news of Demitri's death. Rage began to boil within him. He pressed his hand on his forehead. Ivan looked over and glared at him, but Kain paid him no attention. "Which town the ambush occurred in, we don't know yet. But we do know that the rebellion has spread to at least two other villages. Now, these uprisings seem to have some sort of underlying coordination behind them. Someone must be pulling the strings. There are no grassroots revolutions." Alastor took a deep breath. "With such unrest in the western regions of the Kingdom, it makes us too vulnerable to simply send the full weight of our army, which at the moment is admittedly not much. For if we underestimate the rebels, the impact could be devastating. There is also the fact that we have lost our army's Chief General, my Royal Hand, Sir Drake, at the battle of Grastian." Ivan turned to Kain with his mouth wide open. He then whipped his head back up at King Alastor.

"Then ... who is to be your next hand, my Lord?" Ivan blurted out.

"I will appoint the next hand in time," the King snapped. He glared down at Ivan. "First, I am going to need you two to take all the boys above the age of sixteen and get them as ready for battle as possible. We need numbers, but capable numbers. In the next few days, once we have more intel, we should be able to send a good portion of our men to deal with this insurrection. For now, we must keep the appearance of strength and unity. Say nothing to anyone." The King nodded to the two men as he stood and walked off.

Kain rushed out of the room immediately; he had both hands on his face as he passed through the corridors in disbelief. He returned to his barrack and paced around the room. He banged on his head and breathed in deeply. He sat on the edge of his bed and held his hand on his chest, forcing himself to calm down.

Kain got in bed and tried to go to sleep in order to escape from the reality of what he was enduring. While he laid there, he saw the faces of Demitri and Drake staring at him from the ceiling. After writhing around in his bed, he got up and walked over to his barrel of wine. He held a cup under the nozzle and tapped the barrel.

Kain put the cup to his lips and downed the wine in one gulp. He instantly refilled it and poured it down his throat again. Beginning to feel the relaxation from the alcohol, he sat back down on the edge of his bed. Kain let out a deep sigh and pinched the bridge of his nose while he squeezed his eyes shut. The image of Drake bloody and dying was planted in his head. Kain drank another full cup and soon really started to feel the effects of the alcohol.

Kain then got up, threw his robe on and left his barrack. The cold air calmed him as he walked along the hallway. He looked out over the edge to the city center in the distance. He soon crossed the city square and came to an alleyway which led to the interior of the Capital.

The night had awoken the cretins in the city, and they littered the shadowy corners of the alley. Kain passed through, paying no attention to any of them. Eventually, he found a dark inlet tucked between two larger buildings. He hopped up the couple of steps that led to the door. It was hardly hanging on by its hinges. He pushed aside the crooked and creaky slab of wood and walked into the darkness.

The hallway was thin and long, but when Kain reached the end of it, a bar appeared to his right. The soft light of the candles throughout the room flickered across Kain's face as he took off his hood.

"General Villairo. What can I get you?" the bartender asked. He then smiled softly and set his hands on the counter. The man looked old and weathered. He had hardly any hair left, and what he did have was white, messy and slicked back. A green apron covered the front of him.

"Hey Arthur, a few whiskey shots and a couple of beers how about," Kain whispered as he gave a gentle smile. Arthur nodded and turned to face the wall of liquor behind him.

"I'll bring it over to ya," Arthur said, now reaching for a bottle of liquor.

"Sure. But let me get the shots right here," Kain insisted. He pulled some coins from the pouch in his robes and set them down. Arthur filled three glasses of whiskey and pushed them across the counter.

Kain picked up the first shot and threw it back. He then went down the line until all three glasses were empty. He put his fist to his mouth and burped.

"Let me get one more up here," Kain said as he let out a sigh of relief. Arthur nodded and refilled one of the glasses. Kain downed it, then turned and went to find a seat.

Kain slipped into the wooden booth where he usually sat. It was right up against the back left corner of the bar. He slouched in his seat and tapped the table in front of him. Soon, Arthur carried over a tray of beers and another whiskey shot.

"Brought you an extra whiskey. You look like you could use it." Kain kept his gaze down and smiled at the bartender's generosity. "Mind if I join you?" Arthur asked.

"Not at all. Here, have one of the beers," Kain offered. He waved his arm, inviting Arthur into the booth across from him.

Arthur set the tray down and slid into the other side of the booth. He grabbed one of the beers, took a drink and then looked sternly across the table. Kain was sipping his beer as he stared down and continued tapping the table.

"What's wrong son?" Arthur asked in a hushed tone. He had a worried look on his face. Kain shook his head slowly while he bit his cheek.

After a few moments of silence, Kain spoke, "We lost Sir Drake at the battle of Grastian." Arthur raised his eyebrows. "And it was my fucking fault too." Kain shut his eyes and chugged his beer. He slammed it down as he clenched his fist. "I was there!" He pressed his thumb into his chest. "If I had just fought Jarin myself, I'd have killed him. And Drake would still be here." Kain rubbed his forehead with his left hand. "How could I let it happen again. Right in front of me …." Kain smacked himself in the head and glared at the ceiling.

"That's awful son, I—" Kain then waved his hand, cutting Arthur off.

"But that's not all," Kain continued. He finally looked across the table and stared at Arthur with his bloodshot eyes. "Demitri's dead too," he gave a cynical smile and looked back down at his drink. Arthur gasped and rubbed his face.

"Oh my god," Arthur whispered as he looked at his cup of beer; his mouth was hanging open. He shook his head and swallowed. Kain slammed his hand on the table.

"And you know what Arthur?" Kain wiped his nose and shut his eyes. "If we had just accepted the God damn surrender from the

Galgarians two fucking years ago, we wouldn't even have needed a draft. And we wouldn't have gone to Grastian. And that fucking war would've been over!" Kain smacked his hand on the table. He smiled and twirled around the beer at the bottom of his cup. "And Demitri would still be alive." He took a sip from the drink and sighed. "And Drake would be too."

"Kain, how in the hell are you holding up?" Arthur asked as he put his hand on his chin.

Kain smiled and tilted his head. "Oh, you know me Arthur. I'm as good as I can ever be."

Arthur narrowed his eyes and stared at Kain before asking, "What do you mean, son?"

Kain picked up his drink, "My pain ..." He stopped talking and chugged his beer until it was gone. He stared at Arthur with no expression on his face. "... Is self-chosen." Arthur stayed silent. He glanced down at the table and pursed his lips.

"Here, you take this one too." Arthur offered, sliding his half drank beer over to Kain. He then got up. "I'll bring you some more in a bit." Kain nodded. He took the extra shot Arthur had brought him and then slumped in his seat while he stared at the table.

After a few hours, Arthur finally came over and told Kain the bar was closing. Kain got up, poured a handful of coins into the jar on the bar counter and walked out the back door.

Kain threw his hood on and stumbled through the alleys of the Capital until he finally reached the city square. He walked across the plaza and up the stairs. Soon he was at the door to his room. He paused outside and looked down to his left. Demitri's door was sealed shut. He closed his eyes and went into his room.

At around the same time that Kain had returned to his barrack, a royal advisor was creeping his way inside the King's chambers.

"Your majesty," the advisor whispered while his head peeked around the door.

"What is it?" the King growled as he rolled over and got out of bed.

"There's been another attack; it's the rebels. More of our occupied troops have been killed," the advisor mumbled.

"Where?" Alastor shouted. The advisor gulped as he watched the King slowly turning toward him. "I said, *'Where!?'*" The vein in Alastor's neck was popping out while he clenched his fists. The King's advisor tugged at his collar.

"At ... Dalwen." The messenger explained.

The King froze with his robe halfway on him. He ordered, "Fetch me Kain and Ivan." Alastor's head then swiveled toward his advisor. His face was swelling with rage. "I said get me Kain and Ivan. *Now!*"

The two men were retrieved from their quarters and brought to the King's palace. They came back to the throne room where King Alastor awaited their arrival. The King stood from his chair as they came closer to him. Kain did his best to keep himself together.

The King spoke, "There has been an attack on Dalwen by the rebels. Without control of this city, it is likely the people of the Capital will soon starve. All our men who previously occupied the town have been killed. If we are not able to recapture the town and regain the steady supply of food from Dalwen, I'm not sure how long the residents of the Capital will continue to remain in order. This has now become a dire threat to our Kingdom. We don't have time to train any new men. Now, you both have expressed to me your wishes to be appointed my next Royal Hand." Kain and Ivan snarled as they flashed looks at each other. "Well, I will make a deal with you. Whoever ends this insurrection and brings me the leaders of this rebellion alive will be granted that honor. From what our informers have told us, there seems to be some type of immediate dispersal at the conclusion of their military actions. Where they go after that, we don't know, but they seem to hide. So don't expect to see a roving band of militia. It's going to take some precision to flush them out." The King looked back and forth at his two generals. "We have sent word to rally men from all our nearest military bases. They are on their way now. You will both be in command of a legion. How you go about tracking down the rebel forces will be at your own individual discretion. You will ride at dawn. Dismissed." The King turned away as Ivan and Kain left the throne room. "And men!" The two turned back to him. "I want them *alive*!" While Kain and Ivan made their way out of the throne room, the King's advisor approached Alastor.

"Your majesty, there is … one more thing," the advisor whispered. He then gulped as the King launched his hand to his throat. The advisor gasped while the King kept his grip firmly on his neck. The advisor choked out, "The man leading this charge … they're saying his name … is Bruce Villairo." The King released his grip on the advisor and stared at the ground.

"Bruce … Villairo?" Alastor whispered to himself.

CHAPTER 15

Kain had just shut his eyes when a knock at his door startled him. The sun was still a few hours away from rising, but he rolled out of bed and slipped into his robe. He squeezed his throbbing head and stumbled over to the door. He unfastened the lock and immediately it was pushed in on him. The King stormed his way inside while his guards remained stationed beside the door.

"Sit down," King Alastor commanded. Kain blinked and shook his head. He tried to rub the grogginess from his eyes. "Tell me about your family, boy." The King seemed deeply agitated as he paced back and forth while keeping a stern gaze locked on his general. Kain squinted and then sat down on the edge of his bed.

"Uh, well, I was raised by my mother and my uncle, and I have a twin brother Bru—" The King slapped Kain across the face before he could finish.

Alastor growled, "You, have a twin brother … and you never told me? Another child of Victor Villairo lives?" The King hunched over and held his trembling fist next to Kain's face.

Kain narrowed his bloodshot eyes and stared off to the side, he

113

gulped before saying, "Um … no one ever asked me, my Lord." The King's glare intensified. He then placed his arms behind his back, stood up and inspected the room.

"Well, it appears your twin has been blessed with a great deal of your family's talent for betrayal." The King explained.

Kain shook his head, looking even more bewildered now. "What do you …?" Kain had trouble making sense of what Alastor was trying to tell him.

Alastor interjected before Kain could finish his thought, "The man leading this rebellion is your brother, Bruce Villairo!" The King's spit spattered all over Kain's face. Their noses were practically touching. Kain's mind raced as he looked around the room.

"Bruce …?" Kain's voice trailed off. He squinted his eyes and scowled.

"Am I right to be concerned that any of this rebelliousness lies within you as well? Or worse, that some familial attachment still lingers?" Alastor questioned. Kain furrowed his brow and looked away from the King.

"No! If—if Bruce has decided to betray the Kingdom, then … he's my enemy too. I want his head as much as you, my Lord. I can promise you that," Kain stated firmly while glancing up at Alastor. The King paused and evaluated Kain's sincerity.

Alastor relaxed slightly and stood upright. His face softened and he now looked somewhat pleased.

"Good. Now, rest up," the King ordered before rushing out the door. Kain fastened his door and then sat back on his bed. He put his head in his hands and slowly pulled them down his face.

"Bruce … what the fuck did you do?" Kain whispered to himself. Then he thought about Demitri. He knew it had to be Bruce's rebellion that was responsible for Demitri's death. He jumped up, grabbed his sword and headed to the training facility.

For the next few hours, Kain tore apart each and every one of the practice dummies throughout the buildings. He slashed ferociously at the sewn-up bodies, imagining they were his brother Bruce the entire time. Slices began to litter the dummies as the anger in him only continued to swell.

Once Kain had annihilated all the dummies throughout the training facility, he marched straight to the military forge under the palace. He walked with a fury that radiated off him. The robe of his hood was slung over his head, and he held his sword at his side while his mind ruminated on the deaths of his friends. Kain marched through the corridors beneath the city until finally reaching a cement archway.

When Kain entered the forge, he doused oil over the coals sitting in the hearth. He grabbed flint and steel and lit the coals. Once the flames were burning hot enough, he put the end of his blade into the hearth. He left it in until it was searing red. He then pulled his sword out and placed it on the anvil. He walked over to a bundle of branding sticks and pulled one out.

Kain held up the branding stick and inspected it. The tip was in the shape of the letter D. He looked down at the red-hot blade resting beneath him. His head trembled as he planted the stick into the top end of his sword. He held it there until the metal stick had molded an imprint of its form into the blade.

Kain plunged his sword into a bucket of water; then he quickly yanked it back. He held it to his eyeline. The D shaped insignia was now pressed into the single-edged blade. Kain stared into the marking on his weapon.

"I promise you both. They will pay for this." Kain whispered.

The sky was now beginning to morph into a deep blue, and Kain headed back to his room to get ready. He put on his boots, slipped on his arm guards, strapped on his chest plate and placed his sword on his back. He looked back at his room one last time. He paused and inspected his reflection in the mirror. He glared at himself before turning away and heading for the city square.

Awaiting Kain in the square were two separate armies standing at attention. Ivan screamed orders to his faction of men as Kain approached. Kain was doing his best to ignore the sound of his rival's voice when the King motioned for each of them to come over to him.

Alastor began to inform Kain and Ivan, "There have been more developments in the time since we last spoke. As I told Kain, the man thought to be responsible for what we are dealing with in the outer villages is his twin brother, Bruce Villairo." Ivan's eye twitched as he heard the news. Then his mouth slowly curled into a devious smile. He carefully turned his head to face Kain. The King continued, "We have also come to believe that the small coastal fishing village of Polissa is being used as a communications base. Our watchtowers have sent word that they have been noticing an unusual number of messenger pigeons flying back and forth from there. Quite strange for the small town." The King paused for a moment. "Now, as I have said before, we know little about their army's operational strategies. Every time we have sent soldiers to investigate after an attack, they can't find anything. They may be blending in with the citizens, hiding throughout multiple towns in the outer villages. In order for you to strike efficiently, you must get a step ahead of them. You need to draw them out. Show no weakness; show no mercy; kill all who stand in your way. The people of this Kingdom need to remember who they serve. And all that we do to keep them safe and secure." The two generals nodded.

"A whole family of traitors. What a surprise," Ivan hissed as the two turned away from the King. Kain grabbed Ivan's throat. Ivan smiled and continued to glare at Kain tauntingly. Kain gnashed his teeth and tightened his grip. "Well, what are you waiting for?" Kain continued to keep Ivan in his grasp. They stared each other down for a few more seconds before Kain let him go and stormed off. "That's what I thought!" Ivan yelled with a smile still on his face. Kain flared his nostrils and clenched his jaw trying to hold back his fury.

"Soldiers, on me!" Kain shouted, raised his arm and then mounted his horse. He lashed his horse's restraints and rode out of the city gates. The army then marched in step behind him. The cavalry men and the Commanders came up to lead the pack alongside Kain.

"General, what's our plan?" a Commander asked. Kain looked to the Commander beside him, and then returned his sights to the horizon.

"We'll go first to Polissa. The King believes the rebel soldiers have been operating their communications from there," Kain ordered.

"But, shouldn't we first retake control of Dalwen? You must know how vital that food supply is to the Capital," the Commander challenged.

"Our first priority is gathering intel on the rebel plans. Knowing Ivan, he'll head to Dalwen first. I'm sure he and his men will be able to reclaim a simple farming town. We'll take it upon ourselves to figure out what the rebels' next move is. Our military intervention needs to be without error. If this isn't dealt with efficiently, it will only lead to further insurrection throughout the Kingdom. We can't afford to make a brash military mistake while trying to smoke them out. We can't give them any advantage." Kain explained.

The Commander remained silent, processing the information. He looked at Kain nervously for a few moments before asking, "Sir, is it true … that the man responsible for this is your brother?"

Kain kept his gaze fixed on the horizon. He then bit the side of his cheek before letting out a deep sigh.

"He's no brother of mine."

CHAPTER 16

Ivan and his army had reached the farmlands of Dalwen after only a few hours of riding north. As the army raced toward the town, the villagers began to panic and take refuge in their homes. Rebel soldiers soon rushed outside, geared up and now ready for battle. They charged toward Ivan and his men, but a few of them broke off from the pack and went running in the opposite direction. Within moments, thick clouds of smoke began rising in the distance.

"The rebels are burning the crop fields! We need to put those fires out! Cavalry men, bypass the soldiers and get to those fields!" Ivan commanded. He then put his head down and snapped at his horse's restraints. He raced toward the rebels. Once he reached them, he jumped down from his horse and began striking down anyone that stood in his way. Ivan's soldiers quickly caught up with him and clashed with the remaining rebels.

Three rebels immediately tried to encircle Ivan who bull rushed the middle soldier and sent him off balance and onto the ground. Ivan turned and stabbed the rebel to his right, ducked a swing for his head, then spun around and sliced the other rebel behind him. The first rebel had stood back up and was now bringing his sword down onto Ivan.

Ivan blocked the overhead swing and once their blades were locked, he disengaged and elbowed the soldier in the face. While the rebel was trying to regain his stance, Ivan took his head off with one clean swipe. The other royal soldiers had taken out the remaining rebels, and once the battle was won, they chained up the few remaining survivors.

Ivan rode over to the crop fields as fast as he could. When he got to the edge of the farm, he saw the entire field had been scorched. Thousands of acres of corn, wheat and barley were now up in flames. Ivan's cavalry men had succeeded in tracking down and killing the excess rebels who had broken off from the pack, but the fires could not be stopped or contained.

The fields had been doused in oil. Ivan stood at the foot of the flames in complete distress. He slowly reached for his sword. Ivan then ripped it from its sheath and drove it up to the neck of one of the Commanders. The Commander stiffened as he began to breathe heavily. Sweat beads formed on his face while he raised his arms in the air.

"I gave you an order William! And this is what you've done? The Capital will starve because of this. Because of you!" Ivan screeched as his gaze pierced through the soul of the Commander. The metal blade of Ivan's sword gleamed against the man's neck.

The Commander shuddered, "General, but the fire had begun before we even arrived; there was nothing I could do."

Ivan ripped his sword aside, slitting the man's throat. The other Commanders and cavalry men froze at the sight of their fellow Commander bleeding out in front of them. The man collapsed to his knees, clutching his bloody neck before finally slumping face first into the dirt.

"Excuses like that won't be sufficient when we are dealing with the starvation of our Capital city! Would anyone else like to offer another explanation?" Ivan motioned his sword to the other soldiers surrounding him. No one made a sound. "Back to the town! Find whatever it is these people are hiding. We need answers now!" The soldiers took off for the village at once. Ivan continued to survey the fire that was now beginning to die out. He knelt down and gripped the ash in his palm as the wind soon blew it into the sky.

Ivan mounted his horse and headed back to the town square. He rode up to another of his Commanders while soldiers rummaged through the village, searching for any information that could lead them to the rebel leaders. He slid down from his horse.

"What have you found Ramsey?" Ivan snapped.

The Commander's hands slightly trembled as he turned to Ivan. He stared at the ground and swallowed before he eventually spoke, "One of the rebels decided to talk before being executed. The King's speculations have been proven correct. Rebels are indeed stationed throughout the Kingdom, disguised as regular citizens. Before military operations, mass communication gets distributed throughout the villages to each faction's leaders. Once they receive the signal, the soldiers congregate, execute their plan, then disappear back into their villages. They don't have the strength to take on our army in combat yet, but they are growing, and apparently fast. It also appears that they keep intel highly compartmentalized with only a select few high-ranking rebels actually knowing any future plans and strategy. That was all they could tell us. Finding these men is going to be a shot in the dark if we continue going town to town retaliating against their previous actions. We need to figure out a way to know what their next step is. Or at least to draw them out. Have them bring the battle to us. We have to get them out in the open."

Ivan pressed his fist to his chin as he listened closely to his Commander. The collected information was useful. Still though, he had no real lead to go on. As Ivan gazed ahead deep in thought, he noticed two young boys walking toward him. They looked like they were brothers, and they were carrying small buckets of water as they passed in front of Ivan. His eyes slowly widened as he stared at them intently. He turned his head over to Ramsey while keeping his eyes on the boys.

"Commander," Ivan said while his gaze remained locked on the two young brothers. "Where is it that Kain Villairo was raised?"

The Commander shook his head slightly and mumbled, "Um … I believe it was Valgard, sir. Out in the prairies. Yes, actually I'm certain it was Valgard."

Ivan smirked. "The western prairies …" Ivan whispered under his breath. "Gather the men. We will ride for Valgard at once." The Commander nodded and began walking away. Ivan called to him once more, "And Ramsey, send a messenger back to the Capital. The news of what happened here today mustn't be delivered by pigeon."

Ramsey turned to face Ivan and nodded. "Right away sir."

It took only a few hours for the messenger sent by Ivan to reach the Capital. Upon the messenger's arrival, he was quickly ushered into the King's throne room. The King's advisors were huddled around the royal throne as the messenger walked farther up the red carpet. Once Alastor took notice of the messenger's presence, he turned from his men and gave a rather pleasant smile to the incoming soldier. The young man knelt before the King.

The King waved his arms and told the man, "Rise! Rise! Tell me now, how many men should be sent to collect the crops? I have fifty on standby. We have twenty carriages prepared for shipment. Will that be enough?" The messenger refused to meet the King's gaze. He stared down at his feet before mustering up the courage to speak.

"Your Majesty, I'm afraid, the crop fields have been destroyed."

"What … what is this? What are you talking about?" The King had lost all his previous pleasantries. He glared at the messenger as he launched out of his throne. "Speak now or I will cut your tongue from your mouth!" Alastor threatened.

"My Lord, upon our arrival, the rebels had already doused the crops with oil. It was ready to burn as soon as we arrived. There was nothing of use that remained once our men got to them." The messenger finished talking but continued to keep his eyes locked on the ground.

The King seemed unusually calm as he responded. "So," he gave a pleasant smile. "You are telling me that nearly the entire food supply of the Capital has been irretrievably destroyed? And the peasants here will undoubtedly starve?"

The messenger relaxed his posture slightly and stood while still averting his eyes from the King's gaze.

The messenger continued, "Yes, my lord. That seems quite likely." As soon as he finished speaking, a dagger came flying through the air and pegged the young messenger in the chest. He looked up in disbelief, and then gasped for breath. His eyes opened wide as he glanced down and saw the dagger that had pierced his heart. He wobbled, then collapsed and hit the ground. Soon his body began to curl up. Blood leaked from him as he slowly quit moving.

The King faced the advisors standing beside him and gave his orders. "Alert the public of a city-wide rationing, to be instituted tonight. All will be allowed just one meal per day. All food must be delivered to the city center by dusk for redistribution. Anyone caught hoarding even a single grain of rice shall be put to death, publicly. In fact, make sure to set that precedence immediately." The King adjourned the meeting and rushed out of the throne room.

CHAPTER 17

I van had traveled throughout the remaining daylight hours and then continued through the night. When his army approached Valgard, the sun had already been up for a couple hours. Many of his men had become delirious from operating on so little sleep. Even still, the sight of the Royal Army marching toward the village petrified the townspeople. One by one they began to trickle cautiously into the roadways to observe the arrival. A crowd soon formed near the entrance to the town square. There didn't appear to be any men fitting the age spectrum of potential rebel soldiers.

As the Royal Army got closer to the mob of citizens, Ivan dismounted his horse and began inspecting the townspeople. He lurked through the crowd as the villagers shivered in fear; all refused to make eye contact with him. Ivan kept his grip on his sword while his eyes searched for weakness within the crowd. Once he had made his rounds through the mob trying to sniff out any undercover rebel soldiers, he addressed the village.

"Men, women, and children of Valgard, come forward now with any and all information you have on this rebellion." Ivan tried to appear pleasant while giving his remarks, but after hearing only silence, his face molded into a scowl. Ivan quickly struck fear in the hearts of the people with his insidious gaze. He patrolled his way through the crowd. Finally, he drew his sword. "It seems … no one will be coming forward willingly. That's alright!" Ivan spun around.

A young girl cautiously stepped out from the crowd. She looked to be about twelve. A white cloak draped over her from her head to her ankles. She looked up at Ivan nervously, then around at the crowd.

"It was … Bruce Villairo, sir. He was the one who started the rebellion." The girls head trembled as she whispered.

"Ah, it looks like we finally have some cooperation. And where is he now, little one?" Ivan asked. The girl fell silent. Ivan glared at the child. He scrunched his eyebrows and gnashed his teeth. *Where is Bruce Villairo!?*" Ivan was now within inches of the little girl's face. His eyes burned with fury. She teared up, but still she remained silent. Ivan brought his sword up to her neck and cut the child's throat. The townspeople gasped as the girl bled out before their eyes. She dropped to her knees and held her throat while blood rushed out.

The townspeople immediately backed away from the girl. Her mother and father cried out in agony, holding their daughter as her skin became ghostly white. Coughs of desperation convulsed her body. Tears streamed down her parents' faces as the girl looked into her parents' eyes and breathed what would be her last breath. The father stared coldly up at Ivan, quickly realizing he was completely powerless to the King's forces.

Ivan returned the father a glare that harbored no empathy. As he was about to further address the crowd, Ivan noticed a hooded figure in the back of the town square slowly making their way out of the mob.

"And where do you think you're going!?" Ivan yelled as he strode over to the figure. They continued forcing their way out of the crowd. Ivan grabbed the arm of the figure and removed their hood. Ivan smiled. "And who might you be?"

The middle-aged woman nervously shook her head as she averted her eyes. "I … well, I'm nobody," she gasped.

"That's who you want! Meredith Villairo, the mother of Bruce!" a man from the crowd shouted. Ivan smiled sinisterly.

Ivan hissed, "Ah, well how wonderful it is to meet you. I've had the unfortunate pleasure of already knowing one of your disgraceful children. Soon I'll have my chance to slay the other."

"Please." Meredith pleaded while she tried resisting Ivan's grip, but he pulled her in closer. She slapped him across the face with her free hand. Ivan looked stunned; then he spat on her.

"I'll never give him up," Meredith promised through gritted teeth. She smiled at Ivan. Ivan released his grip and turned away. He then swung around, coming within inches of her face.

Ivan screamed, "Then you will die a painful and agonizing death!" Ivan grabbed Meredith by the neck and began dragging her to a post beside the wall of men his soldiers had formed. "Miss Villairo here will be burnt alive, and until I get some real information, so will all your children. Men, seize the young ones."

Soldiers invaded the crowd to screams of horror. Ivan tied Meredith to the post while his men littered the floor by her feet with wood and oil. The soldiers had gathered the children into a line next to where Meredith was being held.

Ivan shouted, "Once this filth has turned to ashes, we will simply make our way down this wonderful line. So, parents, I urge you to try and remember what you can, and quickly." Ivan bowed and waved his hand as if he were inviting them into his home. He smiled while he smashed steel onto a stick of flint. Sparks flew and the oil caught fire instantaneously.

Meredith shut her eyes as the flames ignited around her. Tears streamed down her face while her skin began to slowly melt. Her screams echoed well beyond the edges of the town, but soon they began to fade while her corpse continued to burn. Ivan then happily started binding the first child from the long line when a man yelled out in opposition.

"Stop! I'll tell you what you need to know!" A man had emerged from the mob; he held back tears as he stared into his daughter's eyes. Ivan released his grip on the girl.

"So, what is it you'd like to say, peasant?" Ivan asked with a cruel grin on his face.

The man looked around nervously, the stares of his peers were all completely focused on him.

The man gulped and wiped his tears before speaking, "A few of the rebel leaders are on their way to the northern villages. The rebellion hasn't really reached there, not yet at least. They need those men before they can take on the Capital. If you get there first though, you could stop them before the size of their army grows too large." Ivan looked at the man. He held his chin while he thought about what the man had said. He then grabbed the girl by her arm and shoved her next to a group of his men.

Ivan stared at the man and hissed, "Well then, you'll be coming with us. And if you're lying, you'll certainly pay the price. As will your daughter." Ivan turned back to face his soldiers. "We will ride north. Get ready to travel." The soldiers quickly began packing their carriages and preparing for their journey north.

CHAPTER 18

Kain and his army had been marching the entire day after their departure from the Capital. By the afternoon of the following day, they had finally arrived at the western coast. As they came upon the small fishing village of Polissa, they saw that the residents were already gathered outside listening to a man speaking from a podium.

When the villagers of Polissa noticed the Royal Army charging toward them, the man standing beside the podium stopped talking and stepped down from the platform. He made his way through the mob of villagers and came forward to greet the army. Kain pulled up on his horse's collar. The man took a knee as Kain slid off the back of his stallion.

The man seemed optimistic as he began to speak, "Welcome royal soldiers, may I ask what has brought you all to our quiet little town?" The man was short and chubby. His black cloak draped over him as he knelt before Kain. After a few moments of silence, Kain observed the crowd and then looked out over the grassy hill at the white sandy beach beyond the village.

Kain then redirected his attention back to the man and responded, "The rebellion. We require any and all information you have on the matter. As well, bring forth any traitors you are harboring. Cooperation by you and your townspeople will be rewarded." The man fell silent. He nervously glanced around while keeping his eyes fixed on the ground.

"Rebellion?" the man gasped, frantically searching for the next thing to say.

Kain rolled his eyes and answered, "Save the lies. Our watchmen have seen an unusual number of pigeons coming in and out of here. Take me to your postmaster at once." The man kept his gaze down. Kain sighed and glanced over at the villagers standing in front of him. "Citizens. I will ask only once more; direct me to your postmaster, or suffer this man's fate." Kain drew his sword from his back and plunged it down through the man's neck. His lifeless body leaned over as Kain pulled his blade from the man's spine. Kain surveyed the mob once again.

Hands began to flare up throughout the crowd. All fingers pointed toward a small shack on the right side of the main road. Kain and a few of his soldiers started walking in that direction. The shack was small, made of white plaster, and had smoke coming from its chimney. As Kain and his soldiers walked through the door, they saw three young men panicking as they tried to burn and destroy a giant stack of parchment paper sitting on a table beside a fireplace. The men froze and turned away from the stack of papers. They yelled out as they each drew small knives and started running toward Kain and his men.

"Keep them alive," Kain ordered while taking on the first of the assailants. He easily disarmed the man and used the butt of his hilt to knock him unconscious. Kain's soldiers also managed to quickly wrestle the knives away from the other two rebels. Soon after the short fight, the three men were tied up by their hands and feet and placed in the corner of the mailroom.

Kain bent over and rested his hands on his knees while he

interrogated the men, "Now, I think it is fair to say that you men are part of the rebel army?" Kain was met with silence. He then snarled, pulled his dagger out and drove it into the leg of one of the prisoners. The man erupted in screams. "I will not be asking again!" Kain glared at the man as he motioned to do the same to the other leg.

"Yes! Yes! We are a part of the rebel army, please," the man shouted while his eyes were shut tight. The two others looked over and shook their heads, deeply disappointed at the ease of his confession. Kain relaxed and stood. He crossed his arms and smiled.

"If you tell me what you know, you may live," Kain said as he lurked over to the table where a few of the undamaged letters were still sitting. He picked them up and began to read.

The prisoner took a deep breath, rubbed the gash on his leg and said, "I'll tell you all you need to know." The prisoner quickly flashed a confident look and gave a nod to his other fellow captives. As Kain's attention was fixated on the letters, the prisoner continued, "It—it was us who began this rebellion! And it is us three who are its leaders!"

Kain parsed through a few letters from the stack but couldn't find anything of value. He set the papers down and was about to turn away when something caught his eye. The last line of one of the letters read, "Make sure word gets to Ben." Kain held the letter up and inspected it.

"Could this mean his uncle Ben?" Kain asked himself. He looked closer to see if he could identify it as Bruce's writing. It didn't appear to be his handwriting, but it had been so long since he had seen his brother's writing that he couldn't be sure.

"Well?" the prisoner snarled while glaring at Kain with pure resentment in his eyes. Kain stared down at the three men. Kain turned back to face his soldiers.

"Execute them," Kain commanded coldly. The man scoffed and began to yell in protest. Before walking all the way through the door, Kain stopped, peeked inside and added, "In front of the town."

The three men were then dragged by their restraints into the middle of the village and placed on their knees. One of Kain's Commanders announced to the crowd the prisoners' crimes of treason, and one by one their throats were cut. The townspeople silently watched in horror.

Kain glanced around the town before yelling, "Men! Let's head out." As Kain led the march, one of his Commanders rode up next to him.

"General, where is it we're heading?" the Commander asked.

Kain looked ahead, keeping a firm focus on the horizon while replying, "Valgard. We'll march without rest until we arrive." The Commander nodded and fell back into line.

Kain and his men rode through the night, and by dawn the next morning they had come upon his hometown of Valgard. He knew it was unlikely Bruce was still there, but he also knew someone there must be in deep communication with the rebels. Perhaps it truly was his uncle Ben pulling the strings of the rebellion.

Kain's long hair flapped in the wind as he rode into Valgard on his black stallion. His legion of soldiers followed close behind. As the army stormed through the village square, residents gathered outside their homes and shops. Looks of worry and fear washed over the townspeople. Kain restrained his horse as he approached the heart of the town.

Kain then called out to the villagers, "Greetings people of Valgard. The army of King Alastor is here to defend you and this Kingdom from the violent treason which has been tormenting these lands. We have traveled here to collect information on the whereabouts of the rebel army. We know the rebellion was started by Bruce Villairo here in this village. Anyone who helps guide the search for him and his men will be rewarded handsomely." Kain continued riding in circles on his horse. The crowd watched him but still stayed silent. Kain sighed and shook his head. "I would prefer to do this the easy way, without so much death, but if you all disagree with that strategy I can always accommodate." Kain turned back to his men and rolled his eyes.

"Aye, soldier," one of the town bartenders called out. "Your men were already here; we told them all we know." The man felt a startling glare coming from Kain. After a brief pause, Kain turned and addressed his men.

"Soldiers, re-interrogate them." Kain ordered.

Kain left his men to terrorize the citizens and followed a dirt path that led out of the village. When he reached the end of the trail, he found himself staring at his childhood home. He yanked at his horse and came to a stop. As he gulped, a wave of nostalgia overcame him. He had been waiting to see his mother for nearly fifteen years.

Kain slid off his horse and walked up to the door. He stood next to the creaky wooden door and closed his eyes. He paused for a moment and then pushed it in.

When Kain walked inside, he found Ben sitting at the same wooden table Kain had eaten and played at during his early childhood. Ben glanced up from his writing, and Kain was shocked at how much he had aged. His hair and beard had grayed and the wrinkles on his forehead were now much more pronounced. Ben's mouth fell open once he realized he was in the presence of his nephew.

"Kain …? Is that you? What are you …?" Ben gasped while he tilted his head and rubbed his eyes. He was so flustered he couldn't speak.

"Uncle," Kain said while calmly giving a nod to Ben. "I'm looking for my mother. I need you both to tell me everything you know about Bruce and his band of rebels. This rebellion must come to an end. Now."

Ben slowly rose from the table. He closed his open mouth, swallowed, then glared at Kain.

"Well, Kain … It's going to be difficult for you to see your mother," Ben whispered angrily.

"What do you mean?" Kain hissed. "What are you talking about?" His heart began to pound.

"It appears another army has already made their way through this town, Kain. A general of your Royal Army, apparently named Ivan, had your mother, my sister!" Ben pounded his fist on the table as he continued to berate his nephew, "Burnt at the stake two days ago!"

Kain then stumbled and nearly lost his balance, but his panic quickly morphed into rage. He stepped back and caught himself. He regained his balance and then lunged forward and gripped Ben by the throat, pinning him against the wooden support beam on the wall. He glared at his uncle and clenched his jaw tightly. He scrunched his face and trembled, still in a state of shock at what he had heard.

"You, let her die ...?" Kain growled. His eyes began to swell with tears. Kain's grip tightened on Ben's throat while he cocked his head to the side.

"Yes, she's dead." Ben could only choke out the words. "But where were you, Kain? Hm?" Kain released his hold on Ben's neck and began pacing the room. Ben gasped as he slowly regained the ability to breathe. He straightened his collar. "Oh how proud they would be! Your parents," Ben yelled while glaring at his nephew. "Their son, Kain Villairo, doing the bidding of the man who staked his own fathers head on the corner of his castle. The castle you now so valiantly defend!" Ben scowled at Kain. "General Villairo. What a disgrace you've become." Ben scoffed and folded his arms.

Kain grabbed his head with his hands and began to pound it. He stared at the dirt floor beneath him as his mouth hung wide open. He slowly rocked back and forth. He shut his eyes while tears softly rolled down his cheeks.

Ben pleaded with his nephew, "King Alastor has twisted your mind into thinking that I, your mother, and your brother even, are somehow your enemies! Come back to us, Kain. Come back to your family!"

All Kain could picture was Ivan, watching as flames incinerated his mother, and no one doing anything to stop it. Rage now consumed him. He slowly turned his head halfway to his uncle and stared at his feet with a menacing glare. He snatched his sword from his back. He leapt forward and again grabbed Ben by the throat, pinning him back against the beam once more. He held the point of his sword against Ben's throat.

"You … you said you'd protect her…. You promised her. I heard you…." Kain whispered. Small tears continued streaming down his face as he shut his eyes and slowly shook his head. He backed off and turned away. Then he spun around and screamed in Ben's face, "You said you'd protect *me*!" Kain swung his blade and sliced at his uncle's neck. Ben's head hit the floor and rolled as his body went limp and crumbled.

Kain dropped his sword and immediately fell to the ground and began panting. He could hardly breathe. He grabbed his chest while he gasped for air. He got on his knees and began hyperventilating. Kain crawled around as he stared at the floor in disbelief.

Kain managed to drag himself over to the wooden beam and then sat back against it. He looked over to see his uncle's head lying next to his body. Kain put his hands on his face and opened his eyes wide.

"What the fuck have I become?" Kain yelled and pounded on his head with his hands. He looked at his uncle's lifeless body once more and gasped.

After a few minutes, Kain was finally able to take deeper and deeper breaths while he leaned his head back against the wooden beam. He glared at the ceiling and tried to re-center his focus on his mission as he had been taught to do all his life while in the Capital. He scrunched his eyebrows and wiped the tears from his face. He got up to leave, but as he walked toward the door, he looked back one last time.

When Kain scanned the room, his eye caught a piece of parchment sitting on the table. Ben had been writing a letter. Kain moved over to the table and began rummaging through the papers. It was all of Ben's communications between him and the rebels. After searching through them, he found a letter from Bruce sitting beneath the unfinished message Ben had been working on. Kain's eyes lit up.

The note explained that Bruce and his closest men were planning a meeting in the small village of Acton, which sat at the foot of the Casgardian mountain range. He then read Ben's unfinished letter intended for Bruce, which explained the events that had occurred since Ivan visited Valgard. Without having received this letter, Kain knew Bruce and the rebels could not yet be aware of the arrival of Ivan and his men at Valgard, nor the death of his mother. Then Kain was once more struck by the remembrance of his mother's death. As it sank in, he stared at the wall. The feeling of white-hot rage searing in his blood started to bubble up inside him. He tried to restrain his anger as his head and hands trembled. He clenched his fists.

Kain broke free from his emotions, gathered the letters and took off from his old home. He mounted his horse and rushed back to the village. A fresh burst of fury had lit a flame inside of him. He swore to make Ivan pay for what he had done to his mother.

As Kain returned to the town square, he saw the village people being tormented by his soldiers everywhere he looked. The town was in total panic while soldiers tyrannized the villagers. Kain rode up to one of his Commanders.

"Have you found anything of use?" Kain asked.

"General, we've been told the rebels are preparing an attack on the Capital. Should we return home? If this is true, the castle is nearly defenseless." The Commander sounded concerned.

"No, no, it's too early. They don't have the men for it. They're lying to you," Kain said as he began riding away. He then turned back to his Commander. "Burn the village. I don't want to recognize the ashes. Send word to Ivan that we'll rendezvous with their army outside of Acton. But don't mention our time here in Valgard." Kain stared out at the town. "The rebel leaders will be meeting at Acton in three days. I'm not sure if their army will be there too, but if they are, we can join forces with Ivan's men and take them before they're prepared. Spread the word to the men." The Commander nodded. Kain guided his horse away from his soldiers, and then looked back over his shoulder at them. "Now burn it."

As Kain rode away, he felt a disgusted stare cut through him. Alice was glaring at him as if he were the apparition of pure evil. Their eyes locked as he strolled past her. A remembrance of juvenile innocence overtook him. Memories of them as children, and memories of his mother and Bruce ran through his mind. He quickly turned away. He clenched his jaw and stared at the horizon. A single tear streamed down his face.

CHAPTER 19

L ater in the evening, hiding within a cluster of northern villages along the coast, Bruce and a portion of the rebel army awaited their next move. While Bruce sat writing in the attic of the town tavern, a soldier crept through the door and interrupted him. Bruce glanced up from his desk as the man poked his head around the door.

"Sir, a letter for you," the man said. Bruce took the message and removed the paper's binding. The letter was from Alice. She informed him of the events that had occurred over the last couple days in Valgard, along with the Royal Army's plans she had overheard from Kain. Alice explained that there had been an interrogation by the King's army, led by Kain. She told Bruce that the Royal Army knew that the rebels were not actually intending to attack the Capital yet. She also warned him that Kain was somehow aware that Bruce and the other rebel leaders were planning to meet at Acton, and that the Royal Army was in turn planning to ambush them there. She went on to explain that both Meredith and Ben were dead.

Bruce glanced up stoically. He looked around the attic and let out a massive sigh. Then he scowled, realizing that it must have been Kain who had killed their mother and uncle, or at the very least, he was in charge of the men who did it. Before he could even get to the end of the letter, Bruce told the soldier to bring James and Leo to him.

When the two men arrived, Bruce looked back and forth at them while he tapped the table. He then explained, "I have just received word that the King's army is trying to surprise us at Acton. They know about our plans to meet there in three days. I believe that as we speak, they're heading there to meet up with the rest of their men. They're planning to ambush us. But, if we instead leave tomorrow morning, we can make it there before them. This may be the only time we'll have prior knowledge of their plans. If we don't take advantage of this, we'll likely be doomed to fight only on the defensive from here on out."

"Do we have the men for this yet? Do we even stand a chance against their full army?" Leo questioned. He stared at Bruce and bit his cheek, worried about the impulsiveness of the decision.

"As of now, they rightly believe we will not be prepared," Bruce confirmed. "At least in the context of our army's size. But if we can position ourselves properly, we can leverage all their assumptions against them. We can remain in the mountains until nightfall. There's a system of caves in the Casgardian Mountains just outside of Acton. We can hide there while they station themselves in the fields by the village. The caves overlook the meadow. When they're sleeping, we'll come down and take them. We'll strike them with our full force just before the sun comes up." Bruce looked back and forth at James and Leo before continuing to address them, "But remember, we'll have only one shot at this. We'll need the benefit of the night's darkness, as many arrows as our army can carry, and the element of surprise. This isn't a perfect plan, but I don't think we'll get another opportunity like this." Bruce sat back in his chair and crossed his legs.

Bruce knew the fate of the entire rebellion rested upon this battle, and he wasn't all that confident they could win. Still, his emotions had clouded his judgment. Bruce wanted Kain dead for this. He couldn't believe his brother would do such a thing. Even if the rumors of Kain's conquests that he had heard in recent years were in fact true.

James spoke up, "Alright Bruce, if you think this is the best move, I'm with you. But we need to get word to Ambrose and John. I think they're still camped out at Norston waiting for the blacksmith to finish the rest of those arrow tips. I can get a pigeon to them within the next few hours. Should we head out in the morning?" Bruce nodded.

Bruce stroked his beard as he gave the command, "Let's get letters out and sent to every town where we have soldiers hiding. We're going to need all hands-on deck. Once we've gathered everyone at Acton, we'll head up into the caves." The other two men nodded.

James, Leo and Bruce then started scribbling notes on the table. As soon as they finished writing, they attached the letters to pigeons and sent them on their way throughout Nymea. Bruce then went throughout the cluster of villages around them and let the other rebel soldiers know of the plan.

Early the next morning, Bruce and the men he had stationed in the neighboring villages headed toward Acton. After traveling for a little over half a day, they eventually reached the tiny salt mining town of Acton.

Not long after Bruce and his men arrived in Acton, small groups of rebels began to file in over the next few hours. Ambrose, John and their men were the last group to arrive just as evening had set in. Once the entirety of the rebel army had congregated, Bruce led them up into the mountains.

The rebel army hiked up a rugged and rocky trail until they eventually came upon a large, open, flat area. Carved into the face of the mountain were seven shadowy entrances that led into the system of caves within the mountains. Bruce, Ambrose, John, James and Leo walked over to the edge of the cliff and peered at the grassy field below.

"This is likely where the Royal Army will gather," Bruce explained as he waved his hand over the meadow. "They'll be waiting for us, watching the town. But they're not expecting us until two days from now. I'm assuming they'll be trickling in sometime around tomorrow afternoon. We'll hit them the night after they arrive. Their guard will be down." Bruce turned around and surveyed the army of men behind him. "We're going to need to craft catapults and get our hands on some oil. We'll need to recruit carpenters from Acton to help first thing tomorrow morning. I'm sure someone there will have oil we can use as well." Bruce's friends nodded.

Bruce then walked toward the mob of rebels who had spread themselves out along the plateau and shouted out, "Men! As you've been told, the King's army will be approaching Acton soon. It appears they intercepted intel that told them of the meeting between all of us Commanders here at Acton. Well, luckily word got back to us in time that they had been informed of our original plan. With this information allowing us to be a step ahead of them, I believe we will have just one shot to defeat them out there on that field." Bruce gazed at the men before him. They held their heads high as Bruce continued his speech. "It is true that their army is bigger than ours; it is true they are better trained than us; it is even true that their soldiers have seen armies and lands far beyond anything we ourselves can imagine." Bruce was now pacing back and forth with his arms behind his back. "But Alastor forgets what is most important when he sends his forces our way. He forgets that we, unlike those soldiers, have a reason to fight!" The men cheered and banged their swords against their shields. "When the royal forces come knocking at our door, do not forget those that have bled for us to be where we are today. Do not forget what that man they call a king has taken from you. Do not forget all that he will take from you. And most importantly, do not forget why it is that you chose to fight!" The men howled with pride as they continued banging their swords and shields together. Bruce paused for a moment and stared at the ground. He then lifted his head high. "Tomorrow at dawn, we will need to prepare the arsenal. But for now, I need you all to rest up. For you have the fight of your lives ahead of you."

CHAPTER 20

Ivan gave his men no rest as they ventured north from Valgard. They had traveled throughout the entire previous day, eventually reaching the northernmost town on the Nymean peninsula well into the night. Boreas was a quiet village located at the end of the foothills of the Casgardian mountain range. The settlement was only a few hundred feet away from the rough and rocky beaches of the Aspero Ocean.

Just before the army entered the village, Ivan pulled on his horse's restraints. The horse came to an immediate halt which caused the Royal Army to stop suddenly as well.

"Let's hope this town will actually have some decent intel," Ivan whispered while slowly turning his head to the man and his daughter whom he had brought along from Valgard. "For you and your daughter's sake, that is." Ivan flashed a wicked smile and then laughed. The daughter gripped her father's arm tightly while he stroked her hand.

When the army congregated in the center of town, no villagers came out to greet them. The army stood at the ready, watching while

Ivan's head snapped back and forth scanning the town.

Ivan glared at the shacks that surrounded him until finally yelling, "Soldiers! Wake these peasants up!" Men immediately started barging into the doors of the huts surrounding the center of the village. Drowsy and sluggish villagers slowly came outside, all still wearing their sleeping garments. Ivan peered out at them with disgust. He surveyed the crowd. It seemed the only people present were old men, women, and very young children. Once Ivan realized there were no men of fighting age, he seethed with anger. Ivan spun around, grabbed the man from Valgard and began dragging him by his collar. The man's daughter cried out as he was ripped away from her grasp. "My patience has officially run out! Let's make a deal, shall we? If you all can't offer me any type of information on the rebel soldiers, I'll kill each and every one of you!" He then turned to see the man's daughter holding her hands over her mouth and crying. Ivan threw the man to the ground and marched toward her. "Starting with this one!"

"No! Please!" the man pleaded for Ivan to show mercy. "I didn't know they had been here already! I'm begging you. Last I had heard they said they were going north! Please! Take me instead!" He was staring up at Ivan while on his knees begging. Ivan looked aside and pulled the daughter by her arm.

"Ramsey, grab me a stake," Ivan ordered. The Commander froze when he heard Ivan's command. He stared at Ivan with his mouth slightly ajar.

"What for?" the Commander asked cautiously. Ivan growled and clenched his fists. He whipped his head over to face Ramsey.

"To impale the stupid bitch. What else would I need it for you fucking idiot?" Ivan growled. Ramsey tilted his head and stared back at Ivan who had begun to tie the girl's hands.

"Sir … you want to impale her?" Ramsey tried to reason with Ivan, "Surely that punishment is too harsh. There was no way this man could have known the rebels had already arrived. The rebels easily could've gotten here between the time he told us and when we arrived."

Ivan's head trembled as he turned back toward Ramsey. The moonlight shone down on his contorted glare.

Ivan sneered, stared at the ground, and then hissed, "I guess … it looks like I was wrong yet again." Ivan snapped his head up. "Instead, we will be starting with you, Ramsey!"

Ivan drew his sword and charged forward. By the time Ramsey pulled his blade from its sheath, Ivan was already within feet of him. Their blades met instantly as Ramsey planted his foot back to try to secure his positioning. Ivan sliced his sword back and forth while Ramsey tried his best to counter. Their blades finally locked, but Ivan knocked Ramsey in the mouth with his elbow and sent him off balance.

Once Ramsey lost his footing, Ivan slashed down at his thighs. The skin on Ramsey's legs split apart and blood poured out of him. Ramsey dropped his sword and collapsed backwards.

Ivan spun around and looked at his army before yelling out, "Somebody grab me a fucking stake!"

Ramsey screamed in pain, clutching his legs in a panic. Men rushed over to the carriage and pulled out a six-foot-long sharpened piece of wood and stabbed it into the ground.

"Now, you two," Ivan barked. He pointed to the couple of soldiers next to him. "Help me carry him." The three of them picked up Ramsey as he shrieked in agony. The men tossed him up over the spear. The tip of the wood ripped through his gut. Ramsey's body was now suspended halfway down the stake, completely lifeless.

Ivan turned back to the crowd of villagers and shouted, "Now, what is it that you all know about the rebellion? Let's be sure to remember our little deal!" Ivan was met with complete silence. He pressed on his forehead while his body shook with rage. "That's it! Everyone! Inside the church, now! Men, escort these disgusting people in!" Ivan waved his hand at the villagers.

Soldiers rushed toward the crowd and started shoving the townspeople into the wooden church located in the back corner of the town. The villagers cried out while they were shoved through the doors. As soon as everyone was inside, Ivan slammed the doors shut. He then grabbed a wooden rod and jammed the handles together, locking the doors from the outside.

"Burn it all!" Ivan screamed as he threw his hands up and paced around in circles laughing. His head twitched in all directions. "You should have listened to me! I'm always true to my word!" Ivan's men started dumping oil along the outer walls of the church before quickly setting fire to it. "Remember as you die! You asked for this!" Whimpers and desperate pleas called out as the church was lit ablaze. The soldiers stood silently and watched the building burn.

Ivan then spun around, looked back at his men and screamed, "Well? Grab our things! We'll set up camp on the beach!" After the order was given, the soldiers marched toward the beach. Once they reached the rocky shores, they unpacked and spread out. Many of them stared out at the red and orange blaze along the horizon. Soon, it began to die out along with the screams of the townspeople.

Later in the night, Ivan and his Commanders were sitting together in the Commander's tent discussing their next move. While they were meeting, a pigeon flew into their camp and landed beside one of the soldiers. The man took the note and brought it into the Commander's tent immediately.

The soldier stood in the doorway for a moment before speaking, "General Villairo has sent word. He claims he intercepted a letter with intel regarding the rebels' plans. He says the rebel leaders are planning to meet in Acton. He wants our army to rendezvous outside of the town and ambush them as they arrive." Ivan sat listening with his hand on his chin. The other Commanders surrounded him at the table.

"I say we do it," said one of the Commanders as he stood and smacked his hands on the table.

"No way. Concentrate nearly the full strength of the Kingdom just for a few rebel leaders? What do you think will happen next? Their army's size will still be intact. And then we'll have no idea where they are or who's even leading them!" another replied. Arguments began to erupt while Ivan sat motionless.

After a few moments, Ivan finally cut in. "Silence!" The men instantly stopped their chatter and looked over at Ivan who then continued, "We will go." Ivan remained still, sitting in his seat with his legs crossed. His hand gripped his chin. "This flock of sheep will soon dissolve—once the shepherds are no longer there to guide their way. These villagers, these, rebels as you call them, are weak. They are inspired, yes. But remove that inspiration and you remove their very life blood." Ivan then suddenly stood from his chair. "Gather the soldiers at dawn. It won't take us more than a few hours to reach Acton." The Commanders scurried out of the tent and went to rest.

When morning came, Ivan and his commanders began shouting orders to the still tired and delirious soldiers. After rallying the army and dismantling the tents, Ivan mounted his horse and rode over to lead the pack. He turned to his Commander riding alongside him.

Ivan raised his eyebrow and addressed his Commanders, "I trust that when we rendezvous with Villairo's army, you will all remain loyal to me as the sole general." The men looked at each other hesitantly once Ivan finished talking. They then nodded slowly. Ivan inspected their responses. "Good. I sense there may be some … conflicts to be resolved." Ivan laughed, turned his gaze forward and then smiled.

CHAPTER 21

After Kain and his men had left Valgard, they then stopped to rest for the night after only a few hours of traveling north. The following morning, they departed and began their journey to Acton. The legion reached the outskirts of Acton at dusk. While the army marched behind, Kain and his Commanders rode their horses at the front of the pack. Out in the distance, they could see the rocky facade of the Casgardian Mountains glowing orange against the sunset. The thick evergreen trees around them quickly began to thin out, making way for a massive open patch of grass ahead.

Kain narrowed his eyes toward the horizon. Black dots could be seen spread out across the meadow. Kain could just barely see the blood red tents along the far edge of the camp's perimeter. As they closed in on the campground, Kain's heart began to race. The thought of his mother being burnt alive replayed over and over in his mind. He could feel a deep pit stuck in his gut while his blood ran cold. He pictured Ivan standing over his mother's lifeless body, grinning with sickening satisfaction. Kain whipped at his horse's ropes.

The stallion sped up instantly. Kain lowered his head toward the horse's neck and glared at the line of tents. The Commanders behind him looked at each other curiously before doing the same. Soon, the six of them were charging toward the camp. They split through the grounds, startling the resting soldiers that they passed by.

Once the men were almost to the tent, Kain dismounted while his horse was still moving. He hit the ground and stormed toward the tent. His Commanders and a few cavalry soldiers slid off their horse's backs and followed behind him. Kain charged inside. Ivan and his men were sitting around a table observing their battle map. They glanced up at Kain.

Ivan was at the head of the table with his back to the entrance. As Ivan turned in his seat, Kain saw a devious smile form on his face. Ivan stood. Before he could even get out a word, Kain walked up to him, pulled his sword from his back and plunged it through Ivan's chest. He held it still for a few moments, staring into Ivan's wide-open eyes. Kain's face was stone cold. He ripped his sword out while blood seeped from Ivan.

Ivan's smile vanished as he clutched his bloody chest. His energy soon slipped away, and he collapsed. As soon as the others in the room recovered from their initial shock, they drew their swords which spurred Kain's Commanders to do so as well. Kain assumed a battle stance and eyed the room of men around him. He stood perched at the ready with his sword in his hand. Everyone's eyes fluttered around the room.

Kain addressed the tense crowd, "Men, I have no quarrel with any of you. If you wish to fight me over this, that's your choice. But I'll tell you this: You'll likely die. And your deaths will be in the name of honoring a man who cared nothing for you or your lives." Kain stepped forward and tightened his grip on his sword. He then explained, "The woman Ivan executed in the town square of Valgard was my mother. If someone did this to the mother of any of you, I'd expect you to have a similar reaction … even still, I realize he was your general. The choice is yours."

The men across the room cautiously started to relax their stances. Kain kept a scowl on his face as he surveyed the men. After a few moments, the men began to sheath their swords.

One of the men spoke up as the tension began to ease, "Well then? What do you expect us to tell the troops?"

Kain put his sword away, stepped back and then answered, "Tell them the truth. I trained most of the younger men in your army during their time at the academy. I know that they'll remain loyal. So long as you all do as well." He glanced around the room with his hands folded on his waist. "I can't imagine they enjoyed Ivan very much." Some of the men laughed quietly.

"We didn't either," one of the men said.

Kain smiled and continued, "Tomorrow, we'll have finally gotten the man behind all this. I'm sure you're all aware, but I intercepted intel that he and the other ringleaders of this rebellion are planning to meet in the village and solidify plans to attack the Capital. We'll station watchmen inside and around the town to send word when the rebels arrive. I'm not sure if they'll be bringing their army. I can't imagine they would risk bringing a noticeably large legion through these lands." The men around the table stayed silent but nodded their heads as Kain explained the plans. "Even still, it's always better to be over prepared." Kain scanned the room before bowing slightly. "Thank you for being here. It will be my honor to fight beside each of you." Kain turned and left the tent with his regiment's Commanders following behind him.

Kain walked through the field before finally reaching his tent. He brushed the curtains aside and went over to sit on the edge of his bed. He undressed and laid down.

After a few hours of tossing and turning, Kain put his armor back on and began pacing the room. He decided to go for a walk. He brushed the curtain out of the way and walked outside. He looked around the camp before heading toward the moonlight. Sleeping soldiers covered the fields, each lying on a piece of cloth. It was deep into the night at this point, and no other men seemed to be awake.

After reaching the edge of their campground, Kain wandered up the hill beside the field. He approached the watchman who was sitting in a chair along the crest of the hill.

Kain greeted the young man, "Evening, soldier."

The watchman's eyes opened wide as he heard Kain's voice.

"General Villairo, what is it sir?" the young soldier asked nervously. He immediately gripped his sword and straightened his loosely fitting helmet.

"No, no, there's nothing wrong. Just out here for a walk," Kain said quietly as he sat next to the young man. "What's your name, soldier?"

"I'm Gavin … sir."

Kain nodded and smiled.

"Take a rest Gavin. I'll look out for the rest of the night," Kain whispered before patting the soldier on the back. The soldier shook his head, got up from his seat and walked off toward the campground.

Kain took over the watch while the young soldier went to find an open space in the grass. Kain crossed his legs and looked up at the night sky. The moon glistened a ghoulish yellow. Out in the distance, storm clouds loomed. The sky beyond the mountains was a deep, dark gray. The calmness of the night soon began to set in. Kain started getting tired. Not long after sitting down, he shut his eyes.

CHAPTER 22

Only a few hours later, massive flaming projectiles started silently flying down from the mountains. They slammed into the field, waking the royal soldiers and sending them into a panic. The grass quickly caught fire. Soldiers leapt up, looked out at the horizon and saw hordes of men storming down from the mountain. Immediately after the fire balls descended, a heap of arrows filled the sky.

The royal soldiers desperately raced around while the arrows rained down on them. Screams erupted as men were struck across the battlefield. They all tried to reach for their shields to give themselves some type of cover. Confusion and drowsiness shrouded the men's reactions.

The sound of clanking metal from the oncoming army was quickly getting louder and louder. Before long, metallic clashing began to echo from the eastern perimeter of the campgrounds as the two armies collided.

On the other side of the field, Kain awoke to the screams of his men behind him. He looked around deliriously and reached behind his back for his blade. He realized he didn't have it. He glanced down the hill from his steep vantage point and saw the rebel assault coming full force in the opposite direction. Kain shot out of his seat and sprinted back to his tent to get his sword.

Kain rushed inside, grabbed his blade and threw it onto his back. He stormed out of his tent, leapt on his horse and flew toward the action. Rain had begun to pour down, putting out most of the fiery patches in the meadow.

As Kain approached the onslaught, he descended onto the ground and drew his sword. Three rebels instantly tried to swarm him. Kain's blade met the first slash. He knocked the oncoming sword to the side and dug the tip of his blade upward into the man's chin.

The other two rebels on each side of him attempted right-handed swings aimed at Kain's head. He ducked and their swords met. Kain spun in a full rotation and cut the rebels' stomachs open at the waistline. They dropped their swords and fell to the ground, clutching their now exposed guts. Kain looked ahead and made his way further into the middle of the fight.

Although the rebels didn't outnumber them, Kain knew that he and the Royal Army were fighting at a disadvantage. He couldn't afford to lose any more men from this initial surprise. The barrage of arrows had already killed or immobilized a good portion of his army. If Kain's men could slow the tempo, he knew they could handle the rebels.

The darkness had given the rebels a great advantage at first, though dawn was finally beginning to break. Storm clouds still shrouded the skies, but a bright orange and yellow blast of light began to break through the thick storm clouds. Kain knew the rebels' luck was about to run out.

As Kain made his way through the battlefield, a man nearly seven feet tall stepped in front of him with a club in hand. Kain came to an abrupt halt and looked up at his opponent. The man swung his club over his head and brought it down on him. Kain hit the ground and rolled just before it smashed onto him. Kain drew his dagger and stabbed the giant's hand. The giant screamed in pain and dropped his club. The man stood upright and looked at the fresh hole in his hand. Kain ducked and rolled through the massive gap between his legs, turned around and sliced the Achilles' tendons of each of his ankles. The man buckled and fell to the ground as he shrieked in agony. Kain sheathed his dagger, drew his sword from his back and drove it down through the man's neck.

Corpses were now starting to pile up. Based on the bodies he could see, Kain estimated half of his troops had been wiped out. The rebel forces were diminishing just as rapidly though, and Kain was finally closing in on the concentrated line of soldiers pressing toward them.

Two rebels charged toward Kain from up the hill. He could see their balance was off as they ran down toward him. He reached for a spear resting beside him. He picked it up and tossed it. The spear spun sideways and simultaneously hit each of the men square in the face. They fell back with their heads being the first thing to collide with the ground. Kain ran forward and scooped up another sword lying in the grass. He leapt between the fallen soldiers and stuck his dual blades into them. He looked up and saw another man coming for him.

Kain pulled the blades out and dropped the extra sword. With their weapons drawn, Kain and the oncoming rebel soldier began circling each other. The battlefield had thinned substantially at this point. Most of the men were now engaged in one-on-one combat throughout the meadow.

The man stepped forward as Kain exploded into an assault. The soldier desperately tried to parry the swings as Kain's speed picked up. Kain threw down five overhand swings against his opponent's shield and tried to beat him down with sheer force. The rebel was using all his energy to keep blocking the blows, but the force eventually became too great. The man's sword was dislodged from his hand and once the rebel was disarmed, Kain sliced down on his neck. The rebel soldier dropped to his knees as blood gushed from the cut across his neck and chest. Kain swung at him with all his might and ripped the man's head off. Kain stood aside the headless body as he stared down at the bloody skull rolling in the grass.

Kain scanned the horizon and saw a man in bright white armor storming toward him. The sunlight coming from behind him was blinding. Kain put his hand up to block the rays and looked closer at the warrior. He stepped forward cautiously and picked up the sword from the man he had just slain. He sheathed it on his back and jogged toward the man.

When the two men approached each other, they began to slow down; each was hesitant to be the first to engage. The soldier was a little bigger than Kain, as well as a few inches taller. His armor was much thicker too. The white shine from his chest plate gleamed against the rain and the sunlight that was now beaming over the horizon. The opposing soldier stopped suddenly, removed his helmet and tossed it aside. He glared at Kain. After looking carefully at the man, Kain's intense stare morphed. His mouth dropped open slightly and his eyes widened.

"Bruce ..." Kain gasped under his breath as he scowled and scrunched his brow. He then looked down at the imprint on his blade, glanced up and growled.

The rain had drenched Kain at this point; he whipped back his hair and raised his sword. He turned his body and stuck out his left foot. Fury swelled within them both. Bruce yelled out at his brother, swinging his sword in anger. Kain met the blow and their swords crossed. Their faces were pressed nearly nose to nose as they pushed against each other. They disengaged and began circling once more.

Kain channeled his inner fury and swung back at his brother. Their swords beat back and forth. Kain was now pushing Bruce back on his heels as he pressed him. Finally, after a flurry of swings, Bruce slipped from their locked swords and grazed Kain's arm. Bruce backed away and raised his sword. Kain snarled and drew the extra blade from his back.

Bruce pulled out the shield that was slung behind him. He braced his stance to prepare for the dual swords Kain was wielding. Kain then began attacking him at a blindingly fast pace. He spun around and around as his left hand swung high and his right hand swung low. Bruce defended with both his shield and sword trying to block the slashes coming his way.

Bruce held his shield to his face as Kain tried to beat him down with the overwhelming power of his repeated swings. As Kain brought his swords down again and again, Bruce finally stepped forward and plunged his shield into Kain and knocked one of his swords out of his hand. Bruce dropped his shield, and the brothers began trading blows with their lone blades.

After a few more clashes between the two, Bruce shouted, "What did they do to you? How could you murder your own mother?"

Kain backed off. "What? No, Bruce that wasn't—" Bruce reengaged before Kain could finish explaining. They battled ferociously as rain dumped on them. Kain could feel Bruce's anger in every swing, but that only ignited more anger in Kain. Their blades and feet danced back and forth.

Bruce then pressed off their crossed blades and sent a vicious swing across his body at Kain, but Kain sidestepped and sent Bruce off balance and tumbling over. Bruce used his momentum to carry himself into a roll. He regained his footing and picked up the sword Kain had dropped earlier. Now Bruce was fighting with dual swords. Kain had to turn to a defensive strategy. With no shield to utilize, Kain adjusted his stance and started maneuvering through Bruce's strikes.

Kain met the dual blades above his head, and then knelt to pick up Bruce's shield. Kain began swinging the shield as a weapon and stepped forward into Bruce, regaining the offensive. He thrust the shield into his brother, then backed away and spun around. He wound up and sent his shield flying at Bruce, who raised his arms to block the shield. It smacked into Bruce's wrist and knocked their father's sword from his grip.

Bruce lunged at Kain, slashing at his head. Kain quickly sidestepped and took aim for Bruce's neck. Bruce leapt backwards. He stumbled, regained his footing, and then sliced Kain across the arm. Kain yelled in pain before striking back at Bruce. Their swords locked as blood dripped from Kain's gash. Rage consumed Kain.

After a few moments of being locked up, Kain brought their sword tips to the ground. He lifted his right leg and smashed it down on Bruce's blade. The sword dropped from his hands and Kain spun around, knocking Bruce in the face with the hilt of his blade. Bruce fell into the mud. Kain jumped on top of his brother, grabbed a stone from the grass and pounded it into Bruce's head. Bruce laid there motionless as Kain slowly got up.

Kain stared down at his brother, and then he looked to his right where their father's sword was lying. He walked over to it and knelt beside it. He picked it up and held it in his grip, staring into the bronze blade. He glanced back one more time at his brother's unconscious body. He closed his eyes and clenched his jaw. He stood up from his knees and stumbled through the field while holding his father's sword in his hand. The rain continued to soak the battlefield.

Kain pulled some rope from one of their carriages and came back to tie his brother up. Once he finished, he looked around at the devastation of the battle. Hundreds of men were lying dead throughout the muddy hills. The sun had now fully risen over the meadow as the last few rebel soldiers met their end.

Across the field, Kain could see some of his soldiers restraining a few of the remaining rebels. Two of Kain's Commanders rode up to him on horseback.

"General, what would you like us to do with the prisoners?" The Commander asked. Kain looked over and stared into the glaring eyes of his brother Bruce. He turned back to his men.

Kain responded, "Take no prisoners except those wearing the mark of a Commander. Bring them to the tents and chain them up. We'll take them back to the Capital with us."

After the four surviving rebel leaders were shackled, they were placed inside a caged trailer along with Bruce. Kain locked the carriage and yelled out to his soldiers. "Men! Gather the armor off of the dead, but leave their corpses behind."

"General, won't King Alastor want the bodies brought back for a royal burial?" a commander called out. Kain scratched his face and shook his head.

"Honestly," Kain said as he raised his eyebrows and let out a massive sigh. "I'm not sure how this is going to be received by the King. We lost a lot of men out there today. Showing up to the Capital with hundreds of dead bodies doesn't exactly demonstrate 'crushing a rebellion'." The Commander nodded as he looked out at the devastation throughout the field. "And, it's probably best we keep this from the citizens too. We don't want the starving peasants realizing just how weak our forces are right now."

CHAPTER 23

The King had been informed of his army's victory only a few hours before they arrived back at the Capital. The men were met with a royal welcome, but the city was visibly different. The markets were dead and the few citizens that populated the streets looked tired and frail.

After the army strolled in through the castle gates, they were greeted by the small number of soldiers that had been left to guard the Capital city. The soldiers guided their path into the city center. The King appeared graceful in his welcoming, but as soon as he noticed the massive piles of armor being hauled in by the trailers, his expression began to tighten. Kain approached the King and knelt before him.

"My Lord," Kain said, awaiting a response while staring with eyes wide open at Alastor's feet.

"Rise," the King snapped, trying to maintain his composure in front of everyone. He whispered under his breath, "You call this a victory? What have you done? We couldn't face a militia with this many men!" The King nervously scanned what remained of his army. "Get out of my sight. Throne room at dusk!" Kain rose but kept his head bowed. He slowly turned away and marched back to his barrack.

Once Kain got to his room, he took his armor off and grabbed a cup from his shelf. He tapped the barrel of wine in the corner of his room and drew a bath. He got in the tub and laid his back against the edge. He took a deep breath before gulping down the glass of wine.

After scrubbing himself down, Kain got out of the bath and dried off. He put his robe on and headed outside. Once he got to the city center, he looked up and saw that the sun was still an hour or so away from setting. He walked along the cobblestone of the plaza and made his way into the city's interior.

While Kain passed through the narrow and congested alley, peasants sat along the walls of the buildings wrapped in robes and looking distraught. They took no notice as Kain walked by with his hood over his head. Before long he came to the crooked door of the bar. He pushed it open and slipped inside. He walked through the short and dimly lit hallway and soon came upon the bar counter. He leaned up against it.

"Two whiskey shots and a beer," Kain muttered.

Arthur spun around from the wall and narrowed his eyes as he tried to make out the figure standing before him, "Oh yeah, and who's asking for it?" Kain dropped his hood and looked forward. Arthur shook his head, "Oh, it's you … sorry Kain, you know the types of people I get around here. Right away."

Arthur came back with the drinks and set them on the bar. Kain dropped a few golden coins in the jar on the counter. He rested his elbows on the bar and rubbed his face. Then he sighed and shook his head.

"Thank you, Arthur." Kain mumbled as he nodded slightly and took the drink tray. He lurked over to his seat in the back of the room. The bar was especially dark that evening. Shady looking people were tucked away in all the little crevices throughout the shack. Kain tossed the two shots of whiskey down his throat. "Ahhhhh." He held his head back while his mouth stayed open. He took a deep breath, shut his eyes and sighed. After waiting there for a few seconds, Kain grabbed the glass of beer and put it to his lips.

"Look who we have here. General Kain Villairo in the flesh." An unknown voice echoed from the shadows. Kain turned his head and saw three men perched on a small circular table to his left. The man who spoke got out of his seat. "I have a question for you, my Lord." The man stumbled forward and sarcastically bowed as the men behind him laughed. "Do you people even fucking realize what that war has done to us peasants? And now this fucking rebellion. Eh?" Kain's face remained emotionless as he sipped his beer. "My kid hasn't had a meal, in two fucking weeks!" Kain set his cup down. The three men were now all standing and slowly inching their way over to Kain.

Kain tapped his glass on the table and smiled before saying, "Well boys, as you know I'm just the general. You should take it up with the King if you have a fucking problem with your day to day." He grabbed the beer and chugged it. Kain looked across the table at the wall. He was sitting in the same place he and Demitri had sat the night before he was killed. Kain grimaced. The men were still moving toward him. Kain snapped his head to his left. "You know what? Actually, on second thought, it's your lucky day. Just this once, I'd be happy to hear your fucking complaints."

Kain threw his glass across the room. It shattered against the head of a man and knocked him unconscious. The other two charged at Kain. He got up from his seat as one of the men threw a punch at him. Kain ducked, grabbed the back of the man's neck and smashed his head on the table where he had been sitting. The last man standing managed to tackle Kain and knock him over into the wooden booth. Kain kicked the guy off him, and they got back on their feet.

"It's gonna feel real nice doing this to a general."

Kain glared at the man, raised his hands and said, "I can promise you one thing. Today is not your fucking day, pal." The man launched his fist through the air. Kain caught it in his left hand and twisted it. The man screamed as his wrist snapped. Kain grabbed him by the throat with his open hand and lifted him off the ground.

"Please ..." the man choked out while he hung in the air.

Kain tightened his grip and glared at the man whose eyes were now starting to roll into the back of his head. Kain momentarily broke out of his rage and tossed the man aside. The man flew into the wall and collapsed. Kain shut his eyes tightly and pounded his head with his fist. He stood there for a moment and pressed his fist against his forehead.

Kain threw his hood up and stormed toward the exit. He tossed all the coins in his pocket at Arthur and kicked open the door. The sun was setting behind him while he rushed through the alleys of the city and pushed aside anyone in his way. His eyes were bloodshot, and his scowl seemed permanently stuck on his face.

Kain raced across the city square and up the stairs to the balcony. After passing through the doors of the palace, he dropped his hood and walked along the red carpet up to the King's throne. The King stayed silent as he watched Kain approach him. Once Kain got up next to Alastor, he bowed. Alastor looked down from his throne while frowning at Kain.

After almost a full minute of silence, the King finally spoke, "As promised, you have been bestowed the honor of serving me as my Royal Hand." The King paused. Kain stood there awkwardly while staring at Alastor's feet. "Kneel boy." Alastor commanded. Kain slowly dropped to his knee. The King walked down the stairs and pulled his sword from his hip. He tapped Kain on each shoulder with the blade. "Now, rise." Kain stood as the King held out the golden gauntlet. Kain took it and placed it on his hand. "Tomorrow, the prisoners will be executed on the royal balcony. You will stand beside them. We must appear unwavering as we regather and rebuild our forces. We cannot afford to show even a hint of weakness. Faith in this Kingdom must be restored. As my Royal Hand, it is now your duty to bring such faith back to these lands." King Alastor stared down at Kain's bowed head. Kain slowly rose before turning away to leave the throne room.

When Kain got back to his barrack, he took his robe off and sat on his bed. He placed the gauntlet on his bedside table. He then got up and tapped his barrel of wine again. He put the cup to his mouth and started drinking. He gulped down as much as he could manage. Some of the blood red liquid leaked from the corner of his mouth and stained his face. He wiped the stream away and sat back down on his bed. He placed his head in his hands and let out a deep breath. As he looked to his right, his father's sword caught his eye. He picked it up and unsheathed it. The golden trimming on the hilt sparkled when Kain held it up against the light of his candles. He gazed into the blade. His hands began trembling. He reached for the wine and took another massive drink from his cup.

Kain threw the sword aside, got up and stared into his mirror. The scars of battle had been etched into his body. A few unhealed wounds still remained. He looked at his reflection as anger began to swell in him. Kain stared at his hands before opening them wide. His head began to shake as he looked back at himself. He punched the mirror, shattering it and sending shards crashing onto the ground below him. He grabbed his head with both hands. His fist was now bleeding. He started breathing deeply and tried to calm himself. After letting out an anxious sigh, he gulped more wine and laid down trying to rest. He immediately got up, put his robe on and walked out the door.

Kain stumbled through the city until he finally reached the same crooked and creaky door tucked away in the alley. He threw his hood up and crept inside. The deeper into the night it got, the more suspicious characters were drawn to the hole in the wall. Kain slowly inspected the room as he walked up to the counter. Arthur turned to him.

"Kain..." the old man whispered while he looked around nervously. "You should really be careful around these parts of the city right now. After you left today, those drunks you whipped got everyone real riled up. This famine's starting to take a toll on everyone. The things they're saying about King Alastor ..." Kain stayed silent for a moment. He kept his hood up and stared at the old man.

"I appreciate the concern Arthur, but I can handle myself." Kain's eyes had dark bags under them. "Four whiskeys, two beers. Please." Kain ordered. He smacked a handful of coins on the counter.

"Just make sure and watch your back, alright?" Arthur said as he turned and gathered the drinks on a tray.

Kain picked the tray up and walked to the same corner where he had been earlier. He slumped in his seat and downed two of the whiskey shots. He sat staring at the wall across from him. Tears welled in his eyes. He shook his head and drank the next two shots.

Kain drank through the night. At this point, his table was scattered with eight empty shot glasses and five empty beer cups. Kain picked up the last full glass of beer and chugged it. As he set it down, his head began to wobble. He folded his arms on the table and laid his head on them.

CHAPTER 24

Arthur came over and pushed on the hooded figure in the corner. Kain inhaled sharply as his eyes snapped open. The room was as dark as it had been when he came in the night before.

"Arthur, what time of day is it?" Kain asked as he rubbed his eyes and put his hand through his hair. Arthur set a glass of water on the table.

"Well past noon," Arthur said calmly. Kain shook his head and looked around. He was the only person in the bar. He launched from his seat and put his hands over his face. "I didn't want to wake you last night. You looked like you needed the rest."

"Shit." Kain mumbled as he grabbed the cup of water and downed it. "Thank you, Arthur." He reached into his pocket, pulled out some coins and handed them to Arthur.

Kain passed through the bar and went out the front entrance this time. He squinted and raised his hand to block the blinding rays coming from the sun. He threw his hood over his head. He rushed through the city and headed back to his room.

"What the fuck," Kain whispered as he pushed against his door. It was jammed shut. He banged his shoulder into it. Nothing happened. He banged on it again and again until finally it busted open. He scowled and rubbed his shoulder.

Kain walked inside and started putting on his armor. Once his chest plate, arm guards and boots were on, he looked up at his sword. Hanging on the mantle was the same single-edged sword he had forged when he was only twelve years old. The D that he had imprinted in the blade faced toward him. He glanced at the ground and saw his father's sword shining in the corner.

Kain shut his eyes and took a deep breath. He reached down, picked up his father's sword and then sheathed it on his back. He slipped his gauntlet on, pulled open his now broken door and rushed down the hallway.

When Kain reached the palace, the King and his guards were already standing outside on the podium. Kain walked up the stairs and looked at Alastor. Both glared at each other. The King jolted his head back slightly and gave a disgusted look as Kain got closer. The bags under Kain's eyes were glaringly obvious and he reeked of alcohol.

"I was beginning to wonder what was taking you so long," the King snarled while he focused on Kain. "We have the prisoners ready." Alastor turned to his guards. "Ring the bell. The citizens should be gathered by the time Kain gets back here. Kain, go down and escort the prisoners to the balcony." Kain bowed his head slightly.

Kain could hear the deafening ring of the bell behind him as he passed through the palace. He walked down the spiral staircase that led beneath the palace and headed through the cold, dark hallway. Torches illuminated the steel bars of the dungeon in the distance. When he got closer, he noticed a few soldiers standing there.

"General. The prisoners have been stripped and are ready for execution."

Kain nodded to the soldier and then looked on at the five men standing before him. White rags were wrapped around their waists and their hands were tied behind their backs. Strips of cloth ran over their mouths, gagging them. They glared at Kain.

"Good," Kain said as he turned away. The soldiers then whipped the prisoners' backs. The rebel prisoners then walked forward through the hallway. Soon they had reached the spiral staircase that led up to the palace. "Up the stairs. Go." Kain pointed his hand, and the men dragged their feet up the steps. Once they had reached the throne room, Kain went up to the front and turned to face the prisoners.

"We'll wait at the palace doors until we hear the King call for us." Kain ordered. The soldiers nodded. They walked along the blood red carpet and stopped right beside the palace doors. Kain pressed his ear to the wood and waited for Alastor.

"And now! These treasonous prisoners shall finally face, justice!" the King yelled out as Kain pushed the door open. The sun's evening rays shone down on them while Kain escorted the men down the stairs and onto the balcony.

A wooden rack about eight feet tall and fifteen feet wide had been constructed on the balcony. Ropes hung down from the wooden beam. Kain pushed the prisoners forward.

"Get on your knees." Kain commanded. The men got down and the soldiers took off the prisoners' old restraints. The soldiers began tying the rope from the beam around the prisoners' wrists.

The prisoners were now situated in a row, on their knees with their arms suspended up by the ropes of the beam. Kain stood beside them and peered into the crowd below him. All citizens were required to attend. The sluggish and frail mob of people stared up at them apathetically. The boys that had been taken in the draft stood behind the mob of peasants, all of them wearing their training gear.

Some of the royal guards started marching down the stairs from the podium. Soon they lined the edge of the balcony on each side of the wooden rack. The blinding, setting sun was reflected from their golden armor. What few infantry soldiers remained in the aftermath of the war were stationed below along the perimeter of the city square.

Kain looked over at the row of prisoners beside him; the golden gauntlet rested on his waist over his jet-black armor. His face looked as menacing as the lion crest on his chest. Just a few feet away from him, Bruce's arms hung from the ropes while he awaited his execution. One of the soldiers went behind the rack and removed the gag from each prisoner's mouth.

The King stood on the golden podium and inspected the crowd below. He yelled out, "Today, order has been restored!" The mob of peasants stayed silent. "No longer are you, or any of the citizens of the Kingdom of Nymea, in any danger. These men before you, will justly meet their end. You are safe, once more!" The King opened his arms and smiled proudly. He glanced down at the balcony and gave the prisoners a disgusted look. "The heads of these traitors, shall be staked, at the four corners of the city walls, as a warning to all of those fantasizing about such insurgency!"

In that moment, Kain's stoic expression shifted, and his eyes opened wide. He immediately recalled the memory of Ben telling the story of his father's fate when he was a child. He looked over at the King and then back at the ground. His face began to feel hot, sweat streamed down his cheeks while he inhaled deeply. He clutched his chest. His heart was racing.

The executioner stood behind the prisoners while he sharpened his massive blade. The screeching of the metal hurt Kain's ears. He shut his eyes tightly and tilted his head. He put his open hand on his forehead and wiped the sweat from his brow.

When Kain opened his eyes and looked behind him, the executioner was slowly raising his sword above his head. Bruce looked up at Kain one last time. The two brothers' eyes locked. Kain saw the same helpless look Bruce had all those years ago. The very same look Bruce gave Kain just as he was being ripped away from his family. Kain was overcome with memories from their youth. A vision of them laughing and sparring in the meadow flashed before his eyes.

Kain broke out of the flashback completely stunned. He stared down at Bruce and swallowed. Then he looked up at the King. He saw Alastor's evil, bloodlust smile begin to curl in anticipation of his brother's death. The executioner started bringing his sword down. It was aimed at Bruce's neck. Bruce shut his eyes. He opened them as he heard a metallic clash right beside his ear.

Kain's blade had met the blow. He stared up at the executioner who was now looking down at him through his meshed mask. Kain spun off their blades and sliced the executioner's head off. Kain drew his dagger and sent it flying through the air. The dagger shredded the prisoners' restraints before pinning the other side of the wooden beam. Kain reached out and grabbed the falling sword of the beheaded executioner; then he tossed Bruce their father's blade. Kain rushed at the royal guards in front of him.

Bruce jumped up and caught the sword as he watched Kain take on the guards. The freed prisoners leapt at the soldiers with their bare hands. Alastor's nostrils flared while he banged his fist on the podium. He yelled for the few men stationed near him to rush Kain and the other rebels.

Bruce raced forward and engaged the other guards around Kain. The two brothers were now fighting with their backs against each other as they ducked and slashed at the guards. Kain grabbed the helmet of the guard in front of him, lifted it and cut his throat. Blood gushed out as Kain pushed him over the balcony. The two guards attacking Bruce had now backed him into Kain who looked over his shoulder.

"Bruce, duck!" Kain shouted as he bull rushed the guard in front of him and knocked him down. He then spun around and flipped his sword upside down as Bruce dropped to his knee. Kain jammed his blade right through the slit of the guard's helmet.

Once Kain and Bruce had taken care of the guards on the balcony, the brothers glanced up at the podium, then back at each other. They raced forward, passing by Bruce's friends who were just beginning to overcome their set of guards. The two of them rushed to meet the other royal guards now making their way down the stairs.

Bruce led the charge and immediately sliced the first guard apart. He then engaged the next few soldiers. Kain followed behind, jumped up on the railing to bypass Bruce and stabbed his blade down into the soldier at the back of the pack. Kain's sword pierced through a chink in the shoulder of the guard's armor. He ripped it out and shoved the guard to the ground. Then he turned his attention to the next two guardsmen coming down the steps.

King Alastor smacked the podium again as he looked out and saw hordes of civilians beginning to rebel against the few soldiers he had stationed throughout the city square. The boys in their training gear looked stunned, not knowing which side to fight for. Alastor had to get this battle under control if he was to keep what little stability remained in his Kingdom. He drew his sword and began making his way down the stairs. Once Kain finished off the two guards at the base of the staircase, he found the lone King standing right in front of him.

Kain stood with his hands at his side. He growled, then leapt forward. He brought his sword down with full force onto Alastor. The King dropped to his knee as he raised his blade to meet Kain's. Alastor spun around and swung his sword at Kain's ankles. Kain jumped up and repositioned himself. The King rose and the two began circling each other.

"Traitor!" Alastor sneered through gritted teeth. "I was beginning to wonder when your true colors would show."

Kain glared at Alastor before shouting back, "I should've seen through your lies years ago. You only care about your power." Kain clenched his jaw as tears welled in his eyes. "It was you." He stabbed his finger at Alastor. "You who turned me into this. This animal. It was you who turned me against my family, against my father." Kain shook his head. He let his sword hang at his side. "You took everything from me!"

King Alastor smiled, "And that is why it is I who is King." Alastor's smile morphed into a grimace. His teeth shone like the fangs of a wolf as he raised his sword to his ear and stabbed it forward. Kain slashed against the strike so powerfully that it knocked Alastor's blade out of his hand. Kain smiled as Alastor scurried away to pick it up. Kain stared at the ground and laughed. He slowly lifted his head and scowled at the King, then he lifted his blade.

Kain yelled out, "But you see Alastor, this monster you made…" Kain gripped his sword tight. "The only man's blood he craves now, is yours!"

Kain lunged at the King. He swung from all directions as Alastor managed to weave through the attacks. After a rally of slashes, Alastor locked their blades against each other, ripped out a dagger from within his robes and stabbed Kain in his rib cage. Kain screamed and backed away. He reached down and ripped out the knife.

Kain growled and threw the dagger at Alastor's head. The King ducked, repositioned himself and stabbed at Kain. Alastor's blade narrowly missed Kain's neck. Kain then slashed low, ripping at the King's robe but missing his body. They began trading blows once more. Their swords locked; then Alastor pushed them up, disengaged and cut Kain across the chest. The slice ripped apart the black leather that covered Kain's chest plate, exposing the iron beneath it.

Kain launched himself at Alastor. Kain's swings began to come faster and faster as the King gave a wicked smile. Alastor was now stepping back toward the edge of the balcony as Kain pressed him. Kain lunged forward and swung, but he narrowly missed Alastor's shoulder. Alastor dodged and struck his sword at Kain's neck. Kain ducked, got up and punched him in the face with his left hand.

Alastor stumbled back and grabbed his face. His nose was bleeding. He gripped his sword with both hands, raised it above his head and sliced downwards. Kain easily sidestepped and countered with a swing at Alastor's head. The King had to quickly backstep. He lost his balance and Kain took a swipe at Alastor which left a deep gash in his arm.

While Alastor was crouched over, Kain pivoted and kicked the King's right knee in. Alastor buckled and dropped to the ground. Kain sliced at Alastor's hand and knocked his sword away. The King yelled in pain as blood dripped from his hands. Kain reached down with his left arm and gripped Alastor by the throat. The metal of the gauntlet on his hand began cutting into Alastor's neck as Kain lifted him off the ground. Alastor put his hands on the gauntlet and gasped for breath. Kain held him in his grasp as his fury consumed him. He threw Alastor against the edge of the balcony. Alastor slumped over on the ground.

Kain looked down at the King, beaten and on his knees. Kain walked over to him, relaxed his stance and stared at the pathetic man kneeling before him. He wound up his blade and readied his swing. Kain lifted his sword behind his head. While he was outstretched and exposed, the King suddenly snatched a spear from the ground beside him. He leapt forward and thrust it upward, puncturing Kain's stomach.

Kain's eyes widened as he stared into the sinister smile that had formed on King Alastor's face. Kain's sword fell from his hands as he stumbled back. He paused for a moment, then yelled out. He regained his balance and growled in anger once more. He gripped the spear and pulled it farther into him. Alastor was yanked toward Kain who swung his arm around Alastor's neck and gripped him close with all his might. Kain stared coldly into the King's eyes. Neither said a word as Kain pulled them both over the edge of the balcony.

The King yelled out as they tumbled down the nearly thirty-foot fall. Kain crashed on top of the King's body. The two bounced apart as they made contact with the ground. The spear was now fully through Kain's stomach as he laid on his side. Blood gushed from the cracked skull of King Alastor. His body remained lifeless beside Kain. Blood was now pooling around Kain. He coughed in pain. He grabbed the spear inside him with both hands and yanked it out, screaming in agony.

Bruce rushed over to the edge of the balcony. "Kain!" He yelled out as he looked around and searched for a way down. He and his men had slain the rest of the King's guardsmen, and they quickly found the staircase leading down to the pavilion.

Bruce raced down the stairs. He ran over to his brother and knelt beside him. He raised Kain's head off the ground and gripped his brother's hand. Kain could only choke out a few words.

"Bruce ... I didn't ... I didn't kill her. I didn't ..." The brothers gazed into each other's eyes one last time. Kain gave a slight smile as his grip loosened. Bruce smiled back as his brother's hand slipped from his grasp. Kain's head slowly fell to the side until it finally rested softly against the ground. Bruce stared down at the soft smile on his face and closed his brother's eyes.

Bruce removed the gauntlet from Kain's hand and placed their father's sword in his grip. Kain rested on his back while his hands on his chest held the sword. It ran down the center of his body. The bronze blade gleamed in the evening orange light.

Bruce rose from his kneeling position and looked around as he wiped the tears from his eyes. He saw the people of the Capital as well as the legion of young boys successfully fighting back against the rest of the royal soldiers. The mob was too large for what remained of the King's army.

Bruce glanced back at the ground. The King's crown now rested at his feet. He reached down and picked it up. He stared at the crown and admired the shine. He held it in his grasp for nearly a minute before looking back at his dead brother. Bruce inhaled sharply, raised the crown above his head and sent it flying. It hit the wall and shattered onto the blood red cobblestone.

"What now, Bruce?" Ambrose stepped forward.

Bruce sighed and gazed out at the setting sun. "Help me carry him." He said, staring down at his brother once more before turning back to his friends. "We'll bury him in Valgard, out on the farm. So that he can finally come back home."

www.ingramcontent.com/pod-product-compliance
Lightning Source LLC
Chambersburg PA
CBHW051109030726
47504CB00006B/1858